SHERLOCK HOLMES
AND THE
HELLBIRDS

SHERLOCK HOLMES
AND THE
HELLBIRDS

Austin Mitchelson
and
Nicholas Utechin

IAN HENRY PUBLICATIONS
PLAYERS PRESS

First published as
Hellbirds
by
Belmont Tower Books

© copyright Tower Publications, Inc, 1976
© copyright Austin Mitchelson and Nicholas Utechin, 1995

ISBN 0 86025 284 1 (U.K.)

Library of Congress Cataloging-in-Publication Data

Mitchelson, Austin.
    Sherlock Holmes and the hellbirds / by Austin Mitchelson, Nicholas
Utechin.
    160p. 22cm.
        ISBN 0-88734-916-1
        1. Holmes, Sherlock (Fictitious character)--Fiction. 2. Watson, John H.
(Fictitious character)--Fiction. 3. Private investigators--England--Fiction. I.
Utechin, Nicholas. II. Title.
PR6063.I84H4 1995
823'.914--dc20

Printed by
Redwood Books
Kennet House, Kennet Way, Trowbridge, Wiltshire BA14 8RN
for
Ian Henry Publications, Ltd.
20 Park Drive, Romford, Essex RM1 4LH

Published simultaneously in the United Kingdom and
the United States of America

A War of Iron

"Really, Watson, this is too bad!"

I looked across from the breakfast table in some surprise. "What on earth do you mean, Holmes?"

A short and testy laugh came from behind a thick cloud of smoke. "This morning's extraordinary postal delivery, Watson."

"But I noticed nothing special among the letters."

"My point exactly; you have hit the nail on the head. There is nothing in today's post; there has been nothing for the last four months. I am, perhaps, a creature of occasional lethargy, but I think I might fairly have expected some small call upon my abilities."

I put aside my plate and, rising, crossed to my accustomed seat by the fireside. As I settled with the newspaper and scanned the columns of war newsI pondered on how right my friend Mr. Sherlock Holmes was. Upon the outbreak of general hostilities in August, we had both hastened back to London, expecting calls to be made on our various abilities. Holmes had successfully engineered the arrest of the German master-spy, Von Bork, at the beginning of that month, and when war came had naturally made himself available for further service. But a visit to his brother at some secret address in Whitehall had rendered my friend almost speechless with fury.

"We are engaged in a war of iron, Sherlock, not a war of intellect!" Mycroft had told him, and that had been the end of a somewhat heated discussion. Praise had been lavished on Holmes's head for the capture of the German agent, but since then my friend had lain mute in Baker Street, permitting himself the occasional solace of a dinner at Frascati's, but in no way able to indulge in his amazing powers.

I myself had been similarly humiliated. Despite my sixty-two years, I had little doubted that my previous wartime experiences would be useful, perhaps in the training of junior military medical officers. Thus I had repaired to the headquarters of my old regiment, the Fifth Northumberland Fusiliers, with whom I had retained contact over all the decades since my own service in Afghanistan. Some kindly things had been said by the commanding officer, but even at the preliminary interview there were indications that my cause would not find favour, and so, indeed, it turned out. Only the previous day, I had received a final letter from Colonel Ellsworthy, leaving me no hope that I could serve my country.

So it was that we found ourselves on that Friday morning, the eighteenth of December, 1914, two elderly and rejected men, restless in Baker Street when we might have hoped to be elsewhere.

While musing on this unhappy inactivity, I had been idly turning the pages of *The Times*. Of a sudden, Holmes's bored voice cut into my reverie. "Anything of interest in the papers, Watson? Give me some flicker of excitement this morning, I beg of you."

I glanced under the Home News columns. "Nothing to tempt you, Holmes, I fear: a brutal robbery of a public house in Ealing, a drab assaulted on the fringes of Whitechapel..."

Holmes waved his fingers impatiently. "For once, Watson, I am not interested in the activities of our petty criminal classes. What news from the front?"

I turned to the relevant page, but another item caught my attention. "Dear Heavens, Holmes, more than one hundred civilians were killed in the disgraceful German naval bombardment of the Yorkshire towns." I referred, of course, to the previous Wednesday's attack on the coastal towns of Whitby and Scarborough. German warships had shelled indiscriminately, and now the full toll was known for the first time.

Holmes wearily inclined his head. "Yes, yes ... but what is the latest from France?"

"Continuing stalemate, it would appear, Holmes. General attacks along the whole length of the front, from Nieuport to Verdun, were ordered by Allied Command on the fourteenth, but no substantial gains have been made so far; the attacks are continuing. 'Our troops have gained ground north of the road from Ypres to Menin ... a reasonable area was cleared of the enemy,' so the correspondent reports."

Holmes snorted in disgust. "'A reasonable area...' indeed! Twenty-five yards, no more, and that is an optimistic assessment. We have entered into a grim period, Watson. There will be no happy return of victorious troops to greet their sweethearts in time for Christmas. The trenches that have been dug along the northern frontier of France will not be filled in for a few years yet, that you can be sure of."

I stared disconsolately at the fire. "But surely, Holmes, our side has had successes enough recently to ensure a German retreat in the near future. Only last month the enemy were forcibly reminded of our Allied strength at Ypres; earlier setbacks, such as that at Mons, are in the past now."

"Do not delude yourself, dear friend," replied Holmes, stretching languidly in his chair. "The course of this war was set in September, when the Germans withdrew from the Marne, with their initial plan of quick destruction of the French armies utterly frustrated. It was clear from that moment that we were involved in a conflict that shall not see its end in four years or more."

We had, of course, held similar conversations over the preceding weeks, but at no time had Holmes been as serious as he was now. All previous experience of war was as nothing compared with the struggles going on at that time in France. The toll of dead and wounded had been terrifyingly high, and Britain, together with her Empire forces and European allies, had had little over which to be enthusiastic since early successes at the Marne, as Holmes had said. For a month after the enemy had retreated to the river Aisne, there had been Allied efforts to dislodge them from the river banks, but none of these, at Aisne itself, at Picardy or Artois, had been crowned with any real success. Telegrams of condolence from the War Office were arriving with frightening constancy at homes throughout the country, and little by little the initial euphoria which had greeted the outbreak of hostilities had dissipated. A week earlier, while Holmes and I had been walking down the Strand after a visit to my publishers, George Newnes of Southampton Street, we had come upon a great crowd gathered outside Charing Cross Station, as a few more thousand men left to go to the front. Both of us had been shocked at the aspect of these men, ready to serve their country, but drawing sadly on their cigarettes as they contemplated their immediate future, clasping their loved ones to them, and gazing forlornly backwards as they pushed towards the trains.

"Come, Watson, we must not wallow. What do you say to a short stroll? This monotonous existence begins to gnaw at me." There was an edge to his voice as he spoke.

It was not long before we found ourselves at the lower end of Baker Street, making our way towards its junction with Oxford Street. We walked in silence, each wrapped in his own thoughts.

"Instructive, but hardly complex," I heard my companion say, and I turned to see him holding a parasol of a particularly violent pink and rolling it over in his hands in meditative fashion.

"Where on earth did you get that, Holmes?" I asked.

"It was leaning against the window of the shoe-maker's we have just passed, and as there was no lady in the shop I deduced accordingly that it had been left earlier in the day. We can drop it in at the police station. Meanwhile we may have some entertainment at its expense. What do you make of it?"

I took it in my hands and examined it. "It would seem to be a parasol...."

"A touch, Watson, a distinct touch!" Holmes commented.

"May I *finish* what I was going to say, Holmes? It is a parasol which has seen rather better days, I fancy: there are several patches. I would hardly judge its owner to be either fashion-conscious or of one of the better classes, because of the uncommonly vulgar colour. Beyond that, I can see nothing." I handed it back to Holmes. "Doubtless you can do better," I added in pointed fashion.

Holmes chuckled. "Oh, indeed yes, my dear fellow, I think I may improve on that. I fear, though, that you are bored now with these demonstrations of my small powers?" He cocked a quizzical eye.

"No, Holmes, proceed," I replied in jocular fashion. "I spoke only as one who has suffered constantly at your hands for thirty years and more."

"Well, with your permission ... you have seen the patches, Watson, but failed to make the obvious inference. Although, as you say, of a lurid colour, this parasol was not cheap when originally purchased: witness the quality of the material, and the Bond Street name engraved on the shaft. No, we can say, therefore, that the owner is a married lady, once rich but no longer so, possessed of a small dog, living in the country, of exceptionally petite and graceful stature, and somewhat forgetful."

I shook my head in disbelief and awaited his explanation.

"That she was once rich," continued Holmes, as we slowly progressed towards Oxford Circus, "is clear, since, as I have said, she purchased this type of parasol when there are others available which are considerably cheaper. That she has fallen upon harder times is just as obvious, since she has been compelled to patch it at various times rather than buy a new one. Her married status is attested by the fact that we have found this object resting outside a man's shoemaker's; the dog is indicated by these marks high up on the ferule - you see the indentations

- some kind of lap-dog, I should imagine. As you can see, the ferule is worn down and somewhat battered, with traces of dried earth engrained in it, indicating habitual walks along country lanes. As to her size, I challenge you, Watson, to slip the tassel on the handle around your wrist. You could hardly get three fingers through it. If her body is built on the same scale as her wrist, she is small indeed. Finally, the mere fact that we are holding her parasol instead of she explains her absent-mindedness. Ah, here is the police station." As he went in to deposit our find, I was left marvelling at the ease with which my friend was able to see where others were blind.

After this short interlude, we continued our silent and pensive walk, turning north at Oxford Circus to join Marylebone Road, and thence back to Baker Street. It was a cool, breezy day, but none of the ravages of winter had yet set in, and it was as pleasant to be outdoors as within on a day such as this. As we approached the steps of 221B, Holmes suddenly gripped my arm.

"Mrs. Hudson is showing someone away from our abode, Watson. Perhaps a visitor for us. Hurry, or we shall miss the young lady."

We hastened forward and reached the door just as Mrs. Hudson was withdrawing and our visitor turning disconsolately away. Holmes raised his hat.

"Sherlock Holmes at your service, my dear lady. Please step inside and let us hope that your train journey from the country will not have been in vain."

The girl, for indeed she can have been no more than fifteen years of age, looked up at Holmes and myself with thankful and, I fancy, tearful eyes, breathed a flustered "Thank you, sir," and stepped back towards the house. As we followed her, Holmes paused an instant and whispered to me. "No Government emissary, I fear, Watson, but the pretty bearer of a pretty problem, I trust." I smiled as we climbed the stairs towards our sitting-room.

Miss Polly Dempster

As our visitor settled herself and prepared to tell her story, I became aware of a great attractiveness, unusual in one so young. Her face was small, but perfectly formed, with two glowing brown eyes which should have been laughing merrily were they not so obviously full of anguish. She clasped and unclasped her hands, looking from Holmes to myself, then burst uncontrollably into tears. I rose immediately to place a sympathetic hand upon her shoulder, but Holmes remained seated, fingers together, and seemingly unconcerned with the plight of our visitor. With the aid of a glass of water, the young girl recovered and was soon able to start her story.

"I beg you to pardon me, gentlemen," she began softly, her voice still breaking with some emotion, "but I had to rise very early this morning in order to be here at this time, and together with my fears over what has happened to my uncle..." She broke off once more, and Holmes leaned forward.

"What is your name, my dear? Pray compose yourself; there is no hurry. Be calm, then tell us what has brought you here in such haste from East Anglia." The young girl looked up at my friend, eyes wide with amazement, but I had not failed to notice the station name of Colchester upon the railway ticket gripped tightly in her hand.

"My name is Polly Dempster, gentlemen, and I do indeed come from a village in Essex. Mr. Holmes, sir, have you ever heard of the Hell Birds of Heaven's Portal?"

Sherlock Holmes stared at Miss Dempster, then slowly shook his head. "Indeed not, my dear. But elucidate, I beg of you. I understand that Heaven's Portal is the name of your village?"

"Yes, sir; it's a small village on the border with Suffolk, and bounded by the sea on the east. I have lived there all my life, and when my parents were both struck down by pneumonia when I was still a small girl, my uncle Ezekial came to the village to look after me. His wife had died a little earlier and he was already retired. And it's my uncle, Mr. Holmes ... my uncle who has ... vanished!" Fresh sobs convulsed her. I offered her my handkerchief and her beautiful young eyes gazed up at me with thanks. I sensed Holmes stiffen in his chair on the far side of the fire and, glancing across, saw a look of extreme boredom cross his face. It was not difficult to see that his ill humour was still with him, and that the case would be rejected out of hand if Miss Dempster did not continue quickly with her tale. He had, I fear, little experience of the emotions of young girls.

"I last saw my uncle, Mr. Ezekial Sloe, two days ago ... that must mean on Wednesday. He left our cottage a little before supper time, saying that he was going to collect some fish from Mr. Parfitt, who owns a boat. I stayed at home, cooking the meal, as I always have. When he did not return in half an hour I began to get a little worried and frightened, because he wasn't usually late for his food. I ran to our neighbour, Mrs. Gamadge, and she was kind and said that Uncle had probably stopped off at an ale-house on his way back from Mr. Parfitt, and would be back soon. But he didn't come back, Mr. Holmes, and he's been gone now for more than forty hours." She paused in her discourse. "And I came to you because I didn't think anyone else could help me. I've read about the marvellous things you can do; there were some old magazines...."

"What are these Hell Birds of which you spoke?" interrupted Holmes sharply.

The girl looked up uneasily. "I believe it's them that have got him - my uncle, I mean. I think they've taken him away..."

"Now, Miss Dempster, we have listened long enough. Will you please pull yourself together, and then tell us of the Birds, who or what they are, and what bearing you believe them to have had on your uncle's disappearance." He spoke in a peremptory tone of voice.

"It's a legend, Mr. Holmes, an old legend of the village; and in recent months, after being forgotten for many years, more and more people who live in Heaven's Portal have said they've seen these Birds. I think the old story goes back to the reign of Queen Elizabeth, or maybe even before. There are twenty great birds, so the legend goes, that have been sent up by the Devil to rule over the village, so that all the inhabitants will be under his power. For more than three hundred years, strange things have happened in the village, and always the older people have shaken their heads and said that the Hell Birds are behind it all. Several people have been found dead, and great birds have been seen flying high above the bodies, their wings spread so wide that they almost blot out the man. For they do their evil master's bidding only in the night. When I was very little, my uncle used to tell me of the Hell

Birds of Heaven's Portal only as a frightening story, when I was misbehaving. But in just the last few months, the Birds have been seen so many times ... so many..." and again the poor girl buried her face in her hands. I shifted uneasily in my chair, but there was little I could do. Holmes seemed to remain unmoved.

"Miss Dempster," he said at length, "you are a brave young girl and I am sorry for you because of your uncle's dis-appearance. I admire you for your action today in coming to London from the coast to see me. But I have had experience of similar cases before now, which were brought before me and attributed to devilish agencies. Watson, you will surely remember the legendary Hound of the Baskerville curse, not to mention the *radix pedis diabolis* whose unpleasant effects we felt in Cornwall so many years ago. It is too facile and, if I may say so, young lady, unworthy of such a sensible mind as yours, to believe in such village gossip. The Hell Birds of Heaven's Portal has an amusing alliterative rhythm, but nothing more to recommend it. Go back to your village, Miss Dempster: you may well find Mr. Sloe at home now, in equal trepidation over your absence as you are over his. It may very well be that, as your worthy neighbour suggested, your uncle went into a public house and there, for reasons known to himself, decided to celebrate in a fashion that has probably left him speechless in a ditch these past two days. No, I don't mean to frighten you," he said in a soothing voice as Polly Dempster stared suddenly up at him, "but I think it is the obvious solution. Has your uncle been known to drink perhaps a little beyond his limits on occasion?" This was not a question which I would have asked a girl of so tender an age, but my friend persisted.

"Well, sir, he has returned the worse for wear sometimes ... that is very true. On his birthday in July, and when we went to war with Germany..." She paused, confused, and lowered her eyes.

"Tut-tut!" cried Holmes in spirited fashion, "Even I have been known to misjudge my capacity for a peculiarly fine brandy; I shall not speak of the doctor here!"

"Really, Holmes, that is entirely uncalled for!" I protested vigorously. "If I do not know my capacity, it is only because I have never reached it."

Holmes waved his hand airily. "I am only trying to make clear to our charming visitor the point that all men at some time or another are apt to behave in this way. I do not say it is right - I only say it occurs. And I am sure, my dear," he said, in a return to the soothing voice, "that this is exactly what has happened to your uncle. Go back to Heaven's Portal, and forget about these extraordinary birds: they do not exist, and a fable born out of ignorance is not worth the attention you are lavishing on it." He smiled at the girl and took her small hand in his. "My, how cold you are, my child. Here is a sovereign; now hasten back to the station - and give my regards to Mr. Sloe on your return."

Miss Dempster seemed reassured by all that Holmes had said, and while I realised that only boredom had made him cut the interview short, I was still aware that his words had the hallmark of truth about them. As the young girl was bidding us farewell, Holmes touched me on the arm.

"Watson, why do you not accompany her to Liverpool Street and buy her a good hearty lunch? She has been a brave girl to come here on her own initiative, and such a distance, and although her plight is not serious, as I think I have indicated, it would be as well for her to be reassured. Avail her of your best bedside manner," he said, with a twinkle in his eye.

The journey across London from Baker Street to the main terminus serving points to East Anglia took no more than a half-hour. The streets were relatively clear, as we had seen on our walk earlier in the morning, save for a small crowd gathered round a broken-down motorised omnibus at Ludgate Circus. Although by this time both Holmes and I were fully able to drive motor cars, we each of us felt that private vehicles were merely obstructions within the city boundaries, and useful only for lengthy, enjoyable excursions into the country. As in the case of the telephone, where Sherlock Holmes was never known to use the object when a telegram would do, so with the automobile. The drivers of hansoms or growlers must surely have sent up a prayer of thanks whenever they saw Sherlock Holmes approach.

At Liverpool Street, Miss Dempster and I lunched well in the Great Eastern Hotel, she seemingly restored to better spirits. From time to time, I was able even to coax a laugh from her, a merry, ringing laugh that turned the eyes of several people towards us. Despite her youth, her beauty and happy prattle almost made me lose track of time, until the sonorous tolling of a City church bell told us that Miss Dempster's train was shortly due to leave. I bade her farewell, enjoined her to fear nothing and to forget any lingering worries over the whereabouts of her uncle, and asked her to visit us again were she ever to be in London at a convenient date. I was quite taken aback when she planted a kiss on my cheek, and was about to be stern with her over the giving of favours to those rather older than herself, but at that instant there was a blast on the engine whistle, and with a great roar and cloud of steam, the train gathered speed. She remained at the window and waved back, until at last I could see her face no more, and turned away from the platform.

"Quite smitten, I see, Watson," said Holmes on my return.

"Not in the least," I replied gruffly. "She is, no doubt, a very pretty young girl, who has the lads of Heaven's Portal at each other's throats. I think she can look on me only as a cheery old grandfather."

"And yet I saw her glancing at you, Watson; ah, these young girls little know the hurt they sometimes do to those older than themselves."

"That is as may be, Holmes," I replied. "I must say, though, that I felt you treated her uncommonly harshly. She was clearly a very scared child on her arrival. She left, it is true, in a happier frame of mind, but that was little due, I think, to what you said."

Holmes turned to the fireplace and dug his hand deep into the Persian slipper, wherein was kept his tobacco. "But her story, my dear Watson, was not only unfeasible, it was preposterous. This is 1914 and there are no Hell Birds anywhere, unless they be in the German trenches on the Western Front. Such stories of devilish birds spiriting away and killing innocent people are absolute nonsense. And if the good men of Heaven's Portal choose to believe in the recent renaissance of such a legend, then the good men of Heaven's Portal are dolts." He lit his pipe and crossed to his desk, prepared for another day of ennui.

The newspapers of the next day were to bring Mr. Ezekial Sloe and his strange disappearance very much to the forefront of our attention.

Inspector Wiggins

Saturday dawned dank and foggy. I breakfasted alone since Sherlock Holmes had of late taken to sleeping through a greater part of the morning. On this occasion he appeared as I was addressing myself to a second portion of devilled kidneys. Still in dressing-gown, he slumped unceremoniously opposite me and disconsolately began leafing through the *Daily Telegraph*.

"Mankind is bent on turning the world into a slaughterhouse," he announced, casting the newspaper violently to the floor. "I cannot tolerate this complete state of inactivity," he cried. "What am I to do, Watson? For God's sake, what am I to do?"

"There is still the matter of Ezekial Sloe..." I suggested.

"Bah!" he sneered. "Am I reduced to seeking out aged drunkards? No, Watson, there must be something better than that."

An idea came to me. "There is something better, Holmes," I said, "and you may look into it this very day."

"Yes, Watson, and what might that be?"

"Why, music, Holmes," I replied. "It is Saturday, and even with this dreadful war there are still concerts in London. Tonight we shall attend a concert."

I was rewarded by an expression of sheer delight on Holmes's face. "Watson, what would I do without you?" he said. "Of course, you are absolutely right. Come, let us find what is available this evening. Pass me the paper."

I retrieved the scattered broadsheet from the rug and assembled it on the table, my friend began a slow perusal of the notices dealing with the evening's musical entertainment. "Mazerelli is conducting at the Wigmore Hall ... a programme of Tchaikovsky at the Æolian. Aha, what's this? Belgian refugees. Interesting."

"What's that about refugees, Holmes?" I said, but there was no reply. Belgian refugees had been flooding into England ever since their tiny nation had been invaded by the Hun at the very beginning of the war, and with them they had brought scandalous reports of the most outrageous atrocities.

"An orchestra made up of musicians who are Belgians and have escaped from the continent is touring England at present," replied Holmes. "It is in aid of the Patriotic Fund. They are playing at various cities around the country before their final concert here in London. The object is to raise funds and, no doubt, heighten everyone's patriotic fervour. It will end with a gala night at the Albert Hall on New Year's Eve before an audience of invited celebrities and Government figures. Doubtless it will be interesting. I may ask Mycroft to arrange an invitation for me."

Holmes paused for a moment. "But tonight I think we shall attend Signor Mazerelli's performance. It is the most promising in a sea of mediocrity . . . but what's this?"

I started, for his careless demeanour of an instant ago had been replaced by the alert, intense manner so familiar to me. I had no idea what could have changed his attitude so dramatically.

"Look for yourself, Watson," said he, his long forefinger indicating a paragraph in the newspaper. It was a report that a body had been found early the previous day at a small village in Essex.

"Why, this must be Ezekial Sloe," I remarked.

"Yes, but read on," said Holmes. I continued the report. "'... no obvious cause of death was immediately apparent,'" said the newspaper, "'but due to the mysterious circumstances surrounding the discovery and condition of the body, Detective Inspector Wiggins of Scotland Yard was immediately despatched to the scene. A doctor who examined the body said that there were numerous small injuries, but none that would have caused death.'"

"That poor child," I remarked.

"What?" exclaimed my friend. "No, Watson, he was more than seventy years... Oh, I see what you mean. Exactly. Poor Miss Dempster." He turned to me. "Nevertheless, you will admit it is an extremely promising case after all. I think it may be necessary to hasten to East Anglia."

"Really, Holmes, you are incorrigible," I protested. "How can you stand before me with what amounts to a smile and describe that poor girl's sad loss as 'extremely promising'? You have already dismissed this affair as relating only to a drunkard."

"Then am I to take it you will not accompany me to Heaven's Portal?" asked my friend.

"Of course I will come with you," I told him, "to death's door if necessary ... but I wish you wouldn't look so damned pleased about it."

Holmes made a small bow in my direction. "You are quite right,

Watson," said he solemnly. "It is a very tragic business." But still there was a merry glint in his eye and an impish grin played at the corners of his mouth.

"Now," he said, "take down the *Bradshaw* and let us see when there is a train for Colchester." I watched Holmes as he studied the timetables, my feelings a mixture of delight that he had been released from his torpor and of sorrow for the plight of Miss Dempster, when there came footsteps upon our stairs.

"Aha!" cried Holmes. "Better and better, Watson. I would know that tread anywhere. It appears the mountain is coming to Mohammed." Our housekeeper, Mrs. Hudson, threw open the door and admitted a familiar face into the sitting-room.

"Wiggins," said Holmes, extending his hand. "Come, what news, what news of Ezekial Sloe?"

Inspector Wiggins strode into the room, throwing off his overcoat and falling into the chair Holmes indicated. "Then you know?" He looked questioningly at Sherlock Holmes.

"Not enough," replied Holmes. "But first you must breakfast, and then you can tell us your story. I see that you have not slept last night, nor eaten either, and you have come straight here from Liverpool Street station. Yet perhaps it is a medical opinion you require more than my own, although I perceive you have had long and earnest discussions with a doctor at the scene of the crime, if crime it was."

Wiggins shook his head in amazement, and even I, who had seen this kind of demonstration on many occasions in the past, was now totally mystified by Holmes's deductions.

My friend held up his hand with a deprecating laugh. "No, please, both of you, no protestations of astonishment, I beg you. I am really going to have to stop this kind of thing. Whenever I make a small observation and deduction of this kind, it takes three times as long to explain it. I sometimes feel it would be more satisfactory if I simply held my tongue. But I will explain. I said that Wiggins had not slept last night. Knowing as we do the investigation he is working on, where he has been, as reported in the morning newspaper, and from his extremely haggard appearance, the darkening under his eyes, the tightening of the skin of the face and the fact that he is wearing what is obviously yesterday's collar, it is not unreasonable to deduce that we have a detective who has not slept all night.

"As to his coming straight here from Liverpool Street station, well, that is a simple matter. As I examined *Bradshaw* not a few moments ago, I noticed that the first train from East Anglia arrives a minute or two before ten in the morning. That would give our friend no time to call anywhere else before arriving here; equally, he would not have had time to eat - which is why we offer him breakfast."

"But you said it might be a medical opinion he was seeking," I interjected. "How can you possibly know that?"

"Two factors," Holmes replied. "Firstly, as I said, it was apparent Wiggins had been in long and earnest discussions with a local doctor or police surgeon. This I knew from a number of tell-tale indications. The first was the piece of sticking plaster on his left hand. It is small enough that it can only be covering a scratch which he would not have bothered with had there not been a medical authority to insist. It is of a type not in general use but kept in hospitals, mortuaries and the like as a protection against infection rather than as bandaging; I use much of it myself when I am dabbling in poisons. Now as even greater proof, Wiggins, there are the distinctive mahogany stains of a certain chemical upon your right cuff. If I am not mistaken, you have been assisting in a test for bloodstains. Since it was I who discovered the test, I am familiar enough with its signs to recognise them instantly."

The years seemed to roll away, and for an instant I recalled my first sight of Sherlock Holmes, almost thirty-five years ago at Barts Hospital. I had been invalided out of the army and was looking for lodgings in London, and my old assistant, Stamford, had introduced me to Holmes. At that first meeting he was in a great state of excitement over discovering this very reaction. "I have found a reagent that is precipitated by hæmoglobin and nothing else," he had shouted delightedly.

But Sherlock Holmes was continuing his discourse. "You will appreciate that such signs indicated that you spent a certain amount of time in company with a doctor. Now, as to whether you want a doctor's opinion or a consultant detective's, I noticed that, tired though you were when you sat down, your eyes kept wandering to my chemical table in the corner. Could the answer to your problem lie there, you were thinking. Your glance then travelled a little way in my direction, halted, and redirected itself towards Dr. Watson."

"Bravo, Holmes," I cried.

My friend made no reply, but walked to the window and looked steadily out into the foggy street. Mrs. Hudson entered and began to clear the breakfast things away, her gaze falling fondly on Wiggins, who had been her favourite for many years. Peter Wiggins had first come to the attention of Sherlock Holmes years before when he was a member of the undisciplined and unschooled band of street arabs which Holmes always referred to as 'the Baker Street division of the detective force' or 'the Baker Street Irregulars'. Wiggins, with little more assistance than the loan of a worn child's reading book, had taught himself to read and write and then had been promoted by Holmes to captain the small band of ragamuffins.

However, my protestations at my friend's use of starving children had had some apparent effect, and when Wiggins was about thirteen years old Holmes had found him lodgings with a motherly East End woman and had arranged for him to attend elementary school. The cost was small, and we were rewarded from time to time by a visit from the lad. Upon leaving his school, young Peter Wiggins had commenced to serve an apprenticeship with a butcher near his adopted home. Again Sherlock Holmes had been responsible for the fees involved. His visits to Baker Street continued, although they grew less frequent; but the boy, growing to manhood, was still a source of pride to Holmes and delight to Mrs. Hudson. To our surprise, after we had not seen Wiggins for some three months, a letter arrived from him one day in 1888. In it he thanked Holmes for all he had done and informed him he had left his master, the butcher, and joined the army. He explained that his ambition was to be, like Holmes, a detective, and until such time as he could fulfil it he felt the army was a better training than a butcher's shop.

Holmes had shaken his head sadly. "If he did but know, Watson, there is little better training for a career as a detective than to be apprenticed to a butcher."

Wiggins had served his term with distinction. In 1896 he was honourably discharged with the rank of Colour Sergeant and the Distinguished Conduct Medal. He had visited us once at Baker Street after his discharge, but it was some years later that we came in contact again - in 1906, in fact, in an adventure which I have chronicled. He had by then achieved his ambition and become a Scotland Yard detective.

My reverie was interrupted as he began to tell the story of the death of Ezekial Sloe. "The body was found early yesterday morning," he began. "The local police considered the circumstances strange, and decided to call in the Yard."

"Young Miss Dempster must have just left for London when the discovery was made," I remarked.

"Yes, Doctor," agreed Wiggins, "but I've never come across anything like this in my life. It's totally inexplicable."

Holmes leaned back in his favourite chair, eyes closed and fingertips together. "Nothing is inexplicable, my dear Wiggins. Pray tell us the circumstances."

"Very well, Mr. Holmes, and I hope you've got an answer, because I'm stumped and that's a fact." He edged forward in his chair. "Ezekial Sloe was reported missing three days ago. He was last seen leaving the Albatross Inn in the village of Heaven's Portal, and he said he was on his way home. Now, the route he was to take led him across a private estate. A public footpath, mind, and only on the edge of the estate, through some woodland. A distance of a mile or so. The footpath commences near the inn and finishes a few yards from Sloe's cottage. The landlord saw Sloe start off along the path, but he never reached the other end. We found his pipe and tobacco pouch a hundred yards or so along there. But his body was found several hundred yards further on."

Holmes nodded. "Excellent, excellent," he muttered, stuffing a handful of shag into the giant bowl of his pipe. "Go on."

"Well, that's all there is to it, really, Mr. Holmes." Wiggins shifted uncomfortably in his seat.

Holmes's eyes opened. "Come, come, Wiggins, you know there is more. Out with it."

"Well," he began reluctantly, "there's a legend locally. The Hell Birds. They're supposed to haunt the wood and the estate where he was found."

"Really, Wiggins," Holmes's voice interrupted icily. "I should have thought you would have known better. Hell Birds, indeed. A fairy tale. And fairy tales have nothing to do with the investigation of crime."

"I know," said Wiggins unhappily, but determined to continue to the end, despite Sherlock Holmes's scorn. "It's just that when we found the body the clothes were all ripped and he was covered with tiny scratch marks and cuts."

A chill filled the room. We sat, all three, in silence for an instant, Holmes leaning forward in his chair totally absorbed in his protégé's gripping story. "Covered, you say?"

Wiggins nodded. "Everywhere. Hands, face, neck, and his clothes were all ripped, as I say."

"Was there no single major injury?"

"No, just superficial scratches."

"Then what did the doctor say? Had the man died from exposure, loss of blood, or what?"

"None of them," replied Wiggins. "The doctor was just as puzzled as I. And he said there was a similar unexplained death some three months ago."

He paused before continuing. "It was as if Sloe had been pecked to death, Mr. Holmes, by a very large bird."

The Tower of London

Minutes later we were in a four-wheeler lurching across London to Liverpool Street station, Sherlock Holmes's eyes glittering with keen interest. Wiggins had been left at Baker Street with instructions to follow on as soon as he had slept and made his report to Scotland Yard. As we hurried across the station concourse, for there were but minutes before the train departed, I was startled to see a gross yet familiar figure stumbling towards us. I drew my friend's attention to the arrival of his elder brother Mycroft.

"Sherlock ... Dr. Watson ... Thank God I was in time to catch you. I attempted to telephone you at Baker Street. Wiggins said you were here."

He halted beside us, his breath coming in great gasps. "I must be seated. Such exertion..." His voice trailed away and Holmes and I sat him down on a convenient bench.

Mycroft Holmes had led a life of absolute inactivity. Holmes had once remarked that Mycroft had his rails - his lodgings, his club and his office in Whitehall. Here then was the result: a man of sixty-seven years so grossly overweight that he was unable to hasten a few steps without severe strain. Nevertheless, whatever his physical shortcomings, he had more than compensated for them with his intellectual achievements. Sherlock Holmes freely admitted that his brother was his superior in the realm of reasoning and deduction, but his inability to seek out his own information had led him in a very different direction from that taken by my friend. Mycroft Holmes, from small beginnings as a Government clerk, had become one of the most influential figures in Whitehall. "There are times when he *is* the Government," Holmes had once remarked. "His is the only brain capable of taking the disparate strands of policy and data and combining them into one overall plan." Now, with the country engaged in war with Germany, Mycroft was more powerful than ever.

Gradually the vast heaving of Mycroft's shoulders, as he fought for breath, ceased, and he was able to speak once more.

"Sherlock, I have grave news," he announced, but was immediately racked by a paroxysm of coughing which prevented further discourse for several minutes.

Sherlock Holmes solemnly waited until his brother could speak once more. "To bring you hot-foot halfway across London, it must be grave news indeed," he said.

Mycroft nodded. "Von Bork. He has escaped from the Tower."

Sherlock Holmes turned away and watched the train for East Anglia as it pulled out of the station.

Mycroft spoke again. "Well, Sherlock? Have you no comment to make?"

My friend rounded on his brother, his face a mask of ill-concealed fury. "Comment, Mycroft? What comment should I have to make? I spent two valuable years hunting down and apprehending the most dangerous man in Europe. I took my life in my hands a dozen times. I travelled halfway across the world and by sheer painstaking effort I ran Von Bork to ground when he was about to leave the country with the very evidence we needed in his baggage.

"Now you come to me and tell me that the Tower of London was not enough to hold the man. That the guards were unable to keep him under lock and key. It is crass ineptitude, Mycroft. Do you now expect me to drop my present case? Do you expect me to dedicate a further two years to hunting Von Bork? Must I pursue this man eternally so that your incompetent underlings can incompetently release him, safe in the knowledge that I will be available to apprehend him yet again?"

Mycroft Holmes, still short of breath, had been unable to speak under his brother's onslaught. Now he took a great gulp of air and cried, "It was not incompetence, Sherlock. It could not be helped."

"Could it not, indeed?" rejoined his brother with heavy sarcasm. "Perhaps your prisoner simply dissolved into thin air?"

"Actually, Sherlock," said Mycroft, "that is exactly what did happen."

Sherlock Holmes showed evident surprise at his brother's answer, and after a moment's thought addressed me. "Heaven's Portal will have to wait, Watson. It seems our services are much in demand suddenly."

We made our way to where Mycroft's chauffeur was waiting with the official conveyance, and, once our baggage was stowed away in the vehicle, we set off for the short drive to the Tower of London.

Our route took us south along Bishopsgate, and soon the grey stone battlements of the massive fortress came into view along with the twin towers of Tower Bridge just beyond. As I gazed from the motor car window a feeling of warmth swept over me as I realised that here was the castle built by the Norman invaders more than eight hundred centuries previously. Those centuries had seen the Tower change from the symbol of domination by the foreign tyrant to a symbol of safety and defiance for the English nation. Now, with war declared against Germany, it was comforting to remember that no hostile army had won a battle on English soil for all those eight hundred years.

Since the outbreak of hostilities the Tower had, to an extent, reverted to its mediæval use, that is, as a state prison. Von Bork, however, had been the only prisoner, although one of his countrymen, a spy by the name of Karl Lody, had spent his last night on earth in the Tower guardroom. Lody had been the subject of a secret trial at the Old Bailey. The sentence had been death by shooting, and on the 5th November he was taken from prison and brought to the Tower. At dawn the next day he was dragged from his cell and marched the few paces to the fortress's indoor miniature rifle range. Popular accounts in the press gave lurid details of the execution, how the white target was placed over Lody's heart, how the firing area was illuminated by electric floodlights, how the German blubbered and begged for mercy as the fateful order was given and how the officer commanding the firing party administered the *coup de grâce* with his revolver.

But with Von Bork, the circumstances were different. He had been lodged in the Tower as a permanent inmate, and the arrangements made for his security were shortly to be revealed to us.

The motor car drew to a halt at the West Gate of the Tower and Mycroft held up a card for inspection by the Yeoman Warder on duty. We were swiftly waved through and our chauffeur, who was clearly familiar with the great fortress, drove directly to a half-timbered house facing out over the notorious lawns known as Tower Green.

"The Queen's House," remarked Mycroft. "At present it does service as accommodation for the military commander here."

I paused a moment after descending from the vehicle and drank in the sombre atmosphere. Facing the Queen's House, on the other side of the Green, was the ancient Norman Keep, the White Tower, built by William the Conqueror and kept as a museum of weaponry and armour for more than two hundred years. At the north end of the lawns stood the small paved area which had been the execution spot. On that site had been placed the block before which two Queens of England had knelt seconds before the axe fell. This place was indeed redolent of the history of England.

A voice cut into my daydreams. "Come, Watson, we must not delay." Clearly Holmes was impatient to deal with the matter before him. As we stepped across the threshold, Holmes paused. "In this very house, Watson," he remarked, "there took place the interrogation of Guy Fawkes and the gunpowder plot conspirators." With that somewhat irrelevant piece of information still hanging in the air he passed into the house, but I realised that he sensed the atmosphere of this historic building as much as I.

Once inside, we were quickly shown to the room used as an office by the military commander of the Tower. Colonel Briland MacWyre thrust out a hand in greeting as Mycroft swiftly effected the introductions. MacWyre was an elderly, ruddy-faced man with the long side-whiskers that had been fashionable some four decades previously.

As soon as we were seated, he addressed himself to Mycroft Holmes. "I hope, sir, that your arrival with these gentlemen does not mean that I am to be held directly responsible for the disappearance of this prisoner?"

He was interrupted by Mycroft. "We are not here to discuss who is responsible for the failure, Colonel MacWyre. We are here to ensure that Von Bork is recaptured before he has an opportunity to communicate with his masters." At this point Mycroft Holmes turned to his brother. "Von Bork was held in the Tower as a prisoner of war, rather than being brought to trial as a spy, because it was vital that he should have no chance to report the information he has back to the German High Command. He is in possession of a secret which, if it were passed on, could set back our war effort by months."

Sherlock Holmes nodded. "In that case, brother, we had better take the necessary steps to apprehend him without delay." He faced MacWyre. "You, sir, had better first inform me of the circumstances in which this man disappeared."

"We discovered he was missing this morning, when a sergeant and I went to wake him," said MacWyre. "His cell was still locked, there was no indication of how he may have left it, yet it was empty. "

"What of the guards through the night?" said Sherlock Holmes.

MacWyre paused. "There are regular patrols both within the fortress and outside the walls," he said. "Furthermore, a sentry was posted outside the block containing Von Bork's cell. No one could have left that building without being seen."

"Are you then saying, Colonel MacWyre, that you had Von Bork locked in his cell last night, placed a sentry at his door and patrolled the outer walls, and yet when you unlocked his door this morning there was no sign of the prisoner or of the means by which he had escaped?" Sherlock Holmes was unable to keep the surprise out of his voice.

The Colonel nodded. "That, Mr. Holmes, is exactly what I am saying. He was there. There is no way he could have got out, but get out he did. There is no explanation."

Sherlock Holmes gave a short laugh. "Never in my experience, Colonel, has there been an event for which there is no explanation. The explanation may at times escape the attention of the inexpert observer, but explanation there always is. In this present matter, of course, there are three distinct possibilities."

MacWyre did not seem impressed. "And they are ... ?" he said.

My friend detailed them on the fingers of one hand. "Firstly, that Von Bork is no longer in the cell. The second possibility, that he is still in the cell, but is not visible. And the third, that he was never there in the first place."

MacWyre turned to Mycroft Holmes. "Really, sir. I don't see that I must remain here and listen to this. I am aware of your brother's respected reputation, but it is apparent that he cannot help in this matter. Please excuse me."

Mycroft halted him with a gesture. "I think you should listen, MacWyre. He is giving you an excellent lesson in the logic of finding something that is missing, be it a sixpence or a German spy."

MacWyre, now very red in the face, started. "But I will not sit in my own office and be told that a prisoner who has escaped was never there in the first place. It is insulting."

"That, sir, was never my intention," said Sherlock Holmes. "I was merely attempting to illustrate that no puzzle is without a solution. However, let us now examine Von Bork's quarters."

It was a short walk from the Commandant's office to the block where the spy had been incarcerated. Our route took us across Tower Green and towards the south walls of the fortress. We approached the part of the building which I recognised as the Bloody Tower where Sir Walter Raleigh had been imprisoned for several years before his eventual execution, and passed beneath the portcullis which could at a moment's notice seal the inner part of the Tower. We were now in a roadway which ran between the inner and outer walls of the Tower of London. Directly in front of the gateway we had used was the infamous Traitors' Gate, through which the murky waters of the river Thames, which bordered this side of the castle, were clearly visible. As we passed by, I noticed a small party of soldiers fishing what appeared to be a piece of cloth from the water.

We arrived at some small buildings huddled against the outer wall. Windows were barred and sentries were still on duty outside. It was apparent that this was the place where Von Bork had been held.

MacWyre spoke. "These buildings are called the Casemates," he said. "They are, in fact, small houses, storerooms, and so on. They continue almost entirely round the outer wall. Here we have a guard-room and several rooms which serve as cells." He paused, and indicated a long low building of painted timber a hundred yards away, still in the narrow avenue between the fortress walls. "The cells are situated so that they are close to that building. It is the miniature rifle range, and is where executions by firing squad take place. Karl Lody was shot there a few weeks ago, as you may have read."

Sherlock Holmes nodded impatiently. "Yes, yes, but that is fast disappearing into history. Let us go inside and see if we can shed any light on the present problem."

The sentry stepped smartly aside and we entered a low-ceilinged, whitewashed room. A sergeant seated at a table in the centre of the floor leaped to attention as the Colonel entered. A few moments later he was demonstrating the arrangements for confining the prisoners. To the right of the door through which we had entered, a corridor led off, containing five cells, although two of these, unlocked, I noticed, were currently in use for storing a variety of materials. On the opposite side of the room there was a stout wooden door which gave on to a similar corridor. However, here, instead of a series of five cells, there were but two rooms placed side by side. Each had a door connecting it with the corridor, but an additional door linked the two rooms. It was here that Von Bork had been incarcerated.

One of the cells had been furnished as a sitting room, the other had been Von Bork's bedroom. There were no windows as such, but each of the cells had a barred skylight.

Sherlock Holmes paced Von Bork's former quarters. "A pretty problem you have, MacWyre," he said. "Tell me the security arrangements."

MacWyre sighed. "The door to the cell which was used as a sitting-room was the only one that could be opened. The other had been locked and then sealed shut with nails. The door between the cells had no lock. The corridor has no other access and the door which connects it with the guard room was bolted except when the sergeant of the guard was making an inspection. At that time he could see through the spy-hole in each of the doors leading to the two cells. The guardroom is staffed at all times by a sergeant, a corporal and three soldiers."

My friend pressed the matter further. "This is no time for reticence, MacWyre. Should you pick up your morning newspapers you will find that England is fighting a desperate and costly war for survival. Men are dying in their thousands each day. You have been charged with the custody of one of this country's greatest enemies. Is your self importance so great that you cannot bring yourself to describe the mechanics of your failure?"

At this the Colonel coloured and took a step towards Holmes. "You, sir, through the influence of your family, may well be in a position to tell me what I should or should not do. But I will not be harried and insulted by any man, whatever position his brother occupies."

Sherlock Holmes regarded the Colonel coolly. "Your bluster, sir, does not excuse your neglect. You will kindly inform me of the circumstances under which you came to lose this prisoner."

MacWyre turned to Mycroft in a silent appeal but the corpulent figure said nothing. Instead, a loose gesture with one arm indicated that MacWyre should do as bidden.

"The sergeant on duty came to look into the cell at seven this morning. I was with him, as there were some questions I had to ask Von Bork," he said, in a voice now quivering with anger. "We looked through the spyhole and could see no movement, and then we opened the door. We entered and found that the prisoner was missing. There was no sign that any of the locks had been forced; and so, on my instructions, the sergeant called the guard and the precincts of the Tower were searched. There was no sign of Von Bork."

Sherlock Holmes nodded slowly. "Very good Colonel. That is absolutely clear. Now call the sergeant."

MacWyre bristled. "Really, sir, I have told you what occurred. Are you doubting my word? If so -" He was interrupted by the sonorous voice of Mycroft Holmes. "Just do as he tells you, MacWyre, there's a good fellow. We really don't have time for your injured pride."

The sergeant was quickly produced, and he smartly recounted the same story as had Colonel MacWyre. Indeed, I was beginning to consider that Holmes, in his fury over the escape of the master spy, was allowing his feelings to be reflected in his attitude towards those entrusted with the task of holding the German.

But the sergeant was adding to his story. "It was clear there was no one in the cell. The Colonel and I searched. He had escaped, sir."

"Quite." Holmes's monosyllabic response clearly worried the sergeant. "What did you do then?"

"The Colonel ordered me to turn out the guard, sir, and I told them to look out for the 'Un - beg pardon, sir, for the prisoner. Then the Colonel and me, we come back in here, sir, and had a look round. Then the Colonel, he says 'The blighter's gone, right enough,' and then he goes off shouting, sir."

My friend nodded. "Thank you, sergeant. A most succinct account. It is, of course, absolutely clear what has happened. Unfortunately, that does not help us to apprehend this man."

MacWyre started "Clear?" he bellowed "If it's that clear, you may like to enlighten me."

Sherlock Holmes turned to the Colonel. "Oh I shouldn't think that is necessary, MacWyre. Surely you are in a position to enlighten us."

For a moment I thought MacWyre was about to strike Holmes. Then he recovered and cried, "I cannot listen to this. I will not accept these insults." As he stepped towards the door the icy voice of Sherlock Holmes interrupted him. "Really, Colonel, I had thought better of you. We do not wish for an unseemly struggle in the public gaze, do we?"

The Colonel paused, then collapsed into a chair. "I knew it could never go undiscovered," he said. "But what choice had I?"

I stared at Sherlock Holmes in utter bewilderment. "But what has happened?" I demanded. "What has occurred here?"

Holmes turned to face us and spoke coldly. "With the connivance of Colonel MacWyre, the most dangerous man in Europe has been let loose. Allow me to explain. Last night Von Bork was confined, as usual, in his cell. This morning he was no longer there. Yet there was no sign of a forced exit. The cell door was locked. And even if it had been forced, what good would it have done the prisoner? He would have gained access only to the corridor outside his cell, a corridor of stone with but one exit, the door to the guardroom. Now, the guardroom is occupied each night by the sergeant, a corporal and three private soldiers, as we have already heard. They were in that room all night, and even if one or two of them had, against regulations, nodded off to sleep, we cannot accept that no one of them would have noticed their only prisoner making his way to freedom.

"You may recall what I said to MacWyre when we first arrived. There are only three possibilities: first, Von Bork was never in the cell. We all know that to be untrue - he was in the cell, and he was locked up last night. Second, he has escaped. That is true. Except that it was impossible for him to have escaped by the time his disappearance was first noted. Consequently, we are left with the third possibility: he was still there, but no one could see him.

"If we accept that as our hypothesis, we are faced with having to explain how it was that no one could see him. He clearly had not made himself totally invisible. Therefore he must have hidden himself somewhere in the rooms." During this discourse my friend had led us back into the bedroom cell. "Now, where could he possibly have hidden? Look around the room, and examine the pillow on the bed. You will see that it is smudged with dust. At some stage it has been on the floor. Glance under the bed as I did a few moments ago, and we have the very hiding place. Dusty, perhaps, but concealed by the counterpane. A man could hide himself there, using the pillow as a necessary comfort, and await the opening of the cell door.

"Following the opening of the door, we have the sergeant and the Colonel entering, the discovery that the prisoner had apparently escaped, the sergeant rushing from the cell and raising the alarm. The next step is that the Colonel has the guard called out and sent to search the grounds of the Tower. Once the hunt moves elsewhere, our fugitive comes out from his hiding place and quickly vacates the cell."

"Certainly, Holmes!" I cried. "But under the bed? Surely that is an obvious place to look?"

Holmes smiled. "Most perceptive, Watson, I shall return to that, but let me proceed for a moment. After leaving the cell Von Bork slips into the guardroom, sees that it has been vacated, and then quickly hides himself in the disused cells opposite. As you know, they are used as storerooms. He finds there an army uniform, which he rapidly dons, and then out he goes to join the hunt for himself."

Mycroft spoke. "But he could not have got out of the Tower, Sherlock. It was sealed within minutes."

Sherlock Holmes shook his head. "You are forgetting, brother, the one entrance that is never guarded. It was there, not a few minutes ago, that we saw a party of men recovering a uniform coat. The key is Traitors' Gate. It is fairly dark in the mornings. Von Bork made his way out of the guardroom wearing a greatcoat, and hastened to Traitors' Gate. There he must have waited for a moment when he could slip into the water unseen, remove the coat and swim to the portcullis. The grating is large enough that a man could easily slip through; from there it is a short, if cold, swim to freedom."

"Marvellous!" I cried. "All this from a few scraps of dust on a pillow."

"That and logic," replied my friend somewhat sharply. "There was no other possible chain of events which could fit the evidence."

"I still say that it was marvellous," I repeated. "But how can you know that Colonel MacWyre was involved?"

"That is another matter," said Sherlock Holmes. "His hostility to the investigation was the first indication that he knew more than he was telling us. I did, however, notice the traces of dust on an otherwise immaculate uniform, which were at first a puzzle. Why, I thought, would a Colonel in the British Army be down on knees and elbows? When we examined the cell it became clear. He had connived with Von Bork in the escape plot. The Colonel knew the prisoner would be hiding under the bed prior to escaping - the obvious hiding place, as you pointed out. He made sure that no one else looked there but he. Then, directing the search away from Traitors' Gate, he gave the prisoner time to collect a uniform which had been left for this precise purpose, and to get clear."

"Of course," said Mycroft. "But why? Why risk his career like that?"

Holmes shrugged. "There could be a thousand reasons," he replied. "But the name MacWyre has an Irish sound to it, and in these times there are those in Ireland who are no sympathizers with the British cause. My supposition would be that in the past MacWyre has allowed a soft heart to persuade him to neglect his duty. One thing has led to another and he finds that now he must obey his enemy's instructions, lest his past misdemeanours be revealed."

And so it was. A short interrogation of the now deflated and repentant colonel produced the truth of the matter. An Irishman, MacWyre had been stationed in Ireland when he had learned that the army were to raid premises suspected of housing revolutionaries. He had discovered that his sister's son was likely to be there, and had secretly passed a message warning the boy to be elsewhere that night. That one indiscretion had led to others, and before he knew what was happening, the revolutionaries were giving orders to the colonel. If he did not obey, they threatened to reveal his assistance to them. Then, when war came, he was a ready-made tool for the Kaiser. The revolutionaries, sympathetic to the German cause, merely told the German secret service of their well-placed victim. He was forced, under threat of exposure, to connive at the escape of Von Bork; they had promised they would leave him in peace after that.

"But of course they would not," Sherlock Holmes's clear voice would not let MacWyre alone with his misery. "Once a blackmailer has you in his clutches, there is nothing that will make him let go. But now you have nothing to lose and everything to gain, whereas before you could only lose. Now that we know what has been happening we can act accordingly. We can, for example, have you tried and executed for treason." Holmes paused to let the import of his words penetrate MacWyre's despair.

The detective continued. "Alternatively, it may be that His Majesty's Government would be satisfied with some lesser penalty ... for example, the immediate resignation of your commission."

I could see the look of hope that flooded into the disgraced soldier's eyes at these words.

Holmes looked directly into MacWyre's face. "Naturally, you would have to prove a new loyalty to the Crown, but if you did that, my brother could guarantee you freedom." Mycroft nodded at this.

MacWyre looked up. "But what must I do?" he implored.

"Just this," said Sherlock Holmes. "Tell us exactly what time Von Bork left the grounds of the Tower, and where he was going."

MacWyre nodded. "That is easy enough, gentlemen. He was free before eight o'clock this morning, and he was picked up in the Pool of

London just a few yards from Traitors' Gate by a boat from the private steam yacht *Ariadne*."

"And where," asked my friend, "was this yacht bound?"

The dreaded answer came back in one word. "Germany. Von Bork was being taken direct to the Kaiser."

Mycroft exploded. "Then we are lost," he cried. "The damage is irreparable, and Von Bork is some six hours ahead of us. He will be approaching the continent by now. By God, MacWyre, England will hear of this if he gets there with his secret! We may have agreed to let you go free, but every history book, every child in school, every man and every woman shall learn that you were the man who traded England for his reputation."

During this tirade, MacWyre had been gesticulating, and I thought he was overcome with emotion. Instead, as Mycroft finished speaking, he cried, "But you are wrong. Von Bork may have escaped six hours ago, but the yacht was not able to leave right away. There had been an accident as a freighter went under Tower Bridge. Her bow clipped one of the stone supports, and the ship slewed broadside across the river. No other shipping was able to pass for hours. Von Bork was trapped in London. His yacht slipped her mooring only a few seconds before you gentlemen arrived here. I watched it from the battlements."

Mycroft consulted an enormous watch which he dragged from his waistcoat pocket. "By George, he's less than an hour ahead of us. He'll still be on the river, and he won't pass Tilbury and be heading out to sea for half-an-hour yet. We can still catch him, Sherlock. Quickly, now."

Leaving a stunned MacWyre under guard, Mycroft hurried to the door and beckoned to his driver, who, knowing his employer's distaste for physical exercise, had followed us in the official motor car. Moments later we were hastening towards Whitehall.

The Secret Depths of Diogenes

Where it was that I expected to be taken I really do not know, but I think the destination least in my mind was the one at which we arrived. The car lurched across London from the City and within minutes we were drawing to a halt outside a familiar stucco-fronted building in St. James's.

"But," I protested to Mycroft, "your club! We were surely heading for your office, to alert the authorities, to tell them the whereabouts of Von Bork ..."

"Enough, Watson," cried Sherlock Holmes crisply. "Out of the car."

My protests brushed aside, I followed the two brothers silently up the steps of the place universally recognised as the strangest club in London, the Diogenes. A number of adventures had brought me here with Sherlock Holmes in the past, when he had felt it necessary to consult what he described as his brother's superior reasoning power. In the Diogenes Club none may speak at all, save in the Strangers' Room, a bow-windowed chamber overlooking St. James's, and it was to this familiar room that I fully expected to be taken. Instead, Mycroft, nodding a silent greeting to the attendants at the door, wearily made his way across the lobby and passed into the cloakroom. Sherlock Holmes and I followed at his heels, and were led out of the cloakroom by what appeared to be a door concealed in the panelling.

We found ourselves in a sizeable stone corridor lit by electricity. Some twenty yards away I espied another attendant in the Diogenes livery holding open a metal door. The three of us were shut into a small room which I realised was a lift, and with a whirring of the electric motor we began to descend.

When the small chamber bumped to a halt almost a full minute later, and the door was opened, an amazing sight met my eyes. We were standing on a gallery surrounding a massive, brightly-lit room. Below us was a huge table covered with a large-scale map of Western Europe, and on the map were pins of different colours indicating, so far as I could judge, not only the positions of our army and navy but also those of the Germans. On the far side of the room were banks of telephones. There must have been a dozen or more, similar to the instrument in our rooms at Baker Street. Even more astonishing, in another part of the room there were half a dozen men, in the uniform of naval ratings, operating wireless equipment. The scene before us was a startling display of scientific precision applied to the art of warfare, and all the more amazing for one who, like myself, had first tasted fire in the Afghan campaign some thirty-six years previously. This was clearly the centre of the British war effort. But, of a sudden, a thought struck me. What was this magnificent establishment doing here, deep underneath the Diogenes Club of all places? Would not the solitude-seeking members notice, and become annoyed at, the constant comings and goings of the staff who manned it?

Mycroft gave that deep, vibrating laugh of his. "Dr. Watson, have you not realised?" he cried, clapping an arm across my shoulders. "This room is the very *raison d'être* of the Diogenes Club. It always has been. A club for men who value absolute privacy? What nonsense! But what better way to allay the suspicions of those who could be enemies? This, Dr. Watson, is the very centre of government. Here we analyze the situation in Europe, indeed the world, and formulate our broad policy. This is something we do in peacetime as well as in war; for the present of course, it has taken on the appearance of a war room. Our sources of information, our agents, all report to their departments and all their data end up here, on the maps, on these charts. It is evaluated and cross-referenced and checked, and we can then recommend the appropriate action for the benefit of the British Empire and to maintain the balance of power in the world."

He broke off abruptly and stalked over to a desk, where a wireless operator stood idle. A message was scribbled down at Mycroft Holmes's dictation, and as the man began pressing up and down on the transmission key the corpulent figure strolled back to us. "I think, gentlemen," he said with a gleam of triumph in his eye, "that we may now take some refreshment."

Sherlock Holmes, who for some minutes had been silently observing the activity in this extraordinary chamber, spoke. "I assume, brother, that you have despatched a radio message to some vessel in the hope that it may be able to apprehend Von Bork's yacht as it attempts to make its way across the North Sea to Germany?"

Mycroft beamed and rubbed his fat hands together in satisfaction. "Oh, more than that, Sherlock." He chuckled as he led us to a small, comfortable furnished room off the gallery. "Much more. I have set into motion a plan which will ensure the apprehension of our opponent."

We seated ourselves in well-padded armchairs and, at a signal from Mycroft, the orderly who had just completed his ministrations with the brandy and soda, drew back the curtains which covered one wall of the room to reveal a window through which we could observe the entire activity in the chamber outside.

"If will observe the chart to the left," said Mycroft Holmes, indicating the far wall, which contained three large boards, in the manner of an hotel owner demonstrating the advantages of his establishment, "you will see that it now contains a large-scale map of the Thames estuary, down which we know that Von Bork is at this moment steaming towards the North Sea and, he hopes, freedom. The red marker at the bottom of the map," Mycroft gazed at each of us in turn to make sure we understood he meant the little wooden boat, "represents Von Bork's yacht. Now, he has to sail almost forty miles from Tower Bridge to the open sea; he then has to make a sea crossing of somewhere between one hundred and two hundred miles, depending on the route he takes, to slip through the British Fleet in the North Sea. What we have done is this: the message which I handed to the wireless operator contained a description of Von Bork, the yacht *Ariadne*, his last known position in the Pool of London, the direction he was heading in, and instructions that he was to be held at all costs. This message will be received by ships of the Royal Navy in the North Sea, together with the relevant security and army units. The ships will immediately steam to the mouth of the Thames to cut off Von Bork's escape. Along the banks of the river we have observers stationed permanently who will report to us as, if and when, they spot the yacht. As each position report comes in, the markers on the map are moved, so that at all times we have the overall position clearly in view."

"Bravo," I cried. "What an absolutely splendid piece of equipment. Why, with information like this and an establishment like this we surely have nothing to fear from the Germans. But if they had had the brains to think up a similar idea, it might he different, eh?"

Mycroft gazed at me for a few seconds and then spoke. "But they do have an establishment which is the very duplicate of this, Dr. Watson."

I started in my seat. "You are sure of that?"

He nodded. "Of course. It was from the Germans that we copied the idea. They thought of it first, you know."

Sherlock Holmes's voice cut in. "Mycroft, it occurs to me that if Von Bork should be less accommodating than we suppose, we might be in some difficulty."

"I think not, Sherlock," replied the elder Holmes. "You are, of course, referring to the possibility that he may decide to leave his craft on the way down river and make his way overland. In the first place, that is extremely unlikely, since the whole escape plot hinged on using the yacht and the river. There has as yet been no development which would alert Von Bork to the possibility that his plan is going awry. But in the unlikely event that he decided to leave his safe conveyance, then the number of observers we have alerted would make it almost certain that such a move would not go undetected. It-would then be a simple matter to flood the area with police and troops, and capture him. But look at the map. He has been spotted."

Our attention was rivetted on the wall opposite. A naval rating using a cane was pushing the red ship to a new position further towards the mouth of the river. Another seaman was at the same time moving other markers, which had been positioned in the North Sea, towards the river mouth. The trap was closing. Time passed, with the markers being shifted a few inches at a time as fresh position reports were either telephoned or sent by wireless to the war room. It was only the clock on the wall and the ominous signals from my stomach which told me it had reached eight in the evening. There was no other way of telling the passing of the hours in that strange cavern deep below that strangest of clubs. Sandwiches were produced as the yacht being used by Von Bork passed Tilbury. It was off Canvey Island when a pot of coffee appeared, and finally the German agent was sailing past the popular beaches of the South End of Prittlewell - the end of the estuary and the beginning of the open sea - when a bottle of whisky arrived before us. At this time the ship markers, representing two ironclads detached from the North Sea blockade, were only inches from the red wedge of wood showing Von Bork's position.

"Surely they must be in sight of each other by now?" I suggested.

But Sherlock Holmes shook his head. "Those few inches on the map represent more than fifteen miles at sea, and the weather is none too clement," and he indicated a board which said simply "Contact area weather-winds gusting to 30 knots, heavy rain, visibility poor." It continued to inform us that the weather in London was equally stormy. A very necessary device in surroundings such as these, I thought; after all, a man leaving this underground cavern would not know whether to wear an Ulster and carry an umbrella or to attire himself in linen jacket and boater unless he had such a report.

Mycroft, who had left our comfortable refuge some minutes before, returned. "We are nearing the time of the confrontation," he said. "I have arranged accommodation at the side of the controller's station, where we may hear the wireless messages that are received from the ships."

We rose and passed through the door to the gallery and then took a few steps down to the floor of the war room. A table was raised on a dais whence the occupants had a clear view of all that was going on. We were led here and seated on some folding chairs which I presumed had been hastily erected for our comfort.

As we three sat down and watched the Lieutenant-Commander who was controlling the operation, I realised that the comparative silence of the room before we entered the observation chamber at the side had now been replaced by a cacophony of telephone bells, crisply-given orders, and a strange kind of chirruping, rather like monotonous song-birds or crickets. "It is the wireless machines receiving reports in Morse code," explained Mycroft

"But can you not listen to a man speak?" I asked. "That was certainly the impression I received from the articles I have read on wireless communication."

Mycroft nodded. "Yes, it can be done, but the equipment is new, not readily available, and cumbersome. Far easier to make use of highly-trained operators who are skilled in the Morse code. I cannot see we shall ever require to hear the actual voice of the person transmitting the message. What would be the point? It is the information we require and nothing else."

Of course he was absolutely correct, but somewhere in my mind was the thought that perhaps some day the voice, and not only the message, would be important. After all, the telephone was making rapid inroads into the use of the telegram. What use might be made of the wireless if it reached that stage? A receiving machine in every room, newspapers of the air, perhaps a wartime battle reported over the wireless as it actually occurred, a dramatic presentation, even.

But a sharp cry broke into my reverie. It was Mycroft Holmes. "They've sighted the yacht," he said, closely studying the despatch. "They're about four miles away."

Sherlock Holmes sat impassive through all this, but I could tell from his attitude that his whole body was rigid with tension. For interminable minutes, we watched the small markers on the map converging. Then the yacht took a new direction and position. "She's spotted the navy," whispered Sherlock Holmes.

The yacht had turned north, heading along the east coast of England, and away from the ships now giving chase. "They must catch her," cried Mycroft. "They have twice her speed." The position of the wall map changed yet again. "They didn't react fast enough," wailed the enormous figure at the top of his voice. "How can they be so remiss?" And, indeed, it seemed as if his anguish was justified the two ironclads assigned to apprehend the yacht seemed to have taken a circuitous route to follow in the small craft's wake.

But it was Sherlock Holmes who reminded us of the true situation. "You must remember," said he, "that you are not seeing a continuous chain of events. We are merely getting reports and attempting to make a reconstruction. Those movements of models are simply moments frozen in time. Who knows what is happening at *this* moment?"

And, true enough, a few seconds later the positions had dramatically altered yet again and the two warships were apparently closing in on their quarry. Another wireless message appeared on the desk. "They have ordered her to heave-to," breathed Mycroft, his bulk quivering in the excitement of the moment.

Yet another wireless operator appeared. "She's ignoring them, sir. Captain requests orders."

Mycroft glared at the rating. "The orders are capture or kill," he bellowed. "No, wait. Tell him to close and board."

"Aye, aye, sir," the rating said, and dashed back to his station. In seconds he was back. "Captain reports yacht heading for coastal shallows; seems to be intending to beach. Impossible to close with her."

Mycroft let loose a string of oaths. "Then tell him this." He scribbled a message on a pad, ripped off the sheet and dropped it on the desk in front of the startled wireless operator. As the paper passed before me, I read the grim words: 'Your orders are capture or kill. Go in and sink. If you cannot pick up all survivors, you must open fire on them. No one must escape.'

The rating read the message and blanched. He seemed about to speak, then, seeing the fury on Mycroft's face, changed his mind and returned to his transmission equipment where he rapidly pounded out the fateful message. A silence fell over the whole room. The receiving equipment ceased its irregular chirping and even the telephones ceased their jangling. No one spoke, but all in the room gave their entire attention to the little wooden ships on the wall map and their occasional movements.

The Commander running the war-room was handed a message. "Both ships have engaged the yacht," he told us. "No further information."

The messages started to come thick and fast again. "Yacht is returning fire with small arms." "She is refusing to stop." "Yacht is afire and sinking." "We are picking up survivors."

"For God's sake, Mycroft," cried Sherlock Holmes, "ask them the obvious question: have they caught Von Bork?"

The flat reply came back almost immediately. "Have not yet identified survivors."

Still later there was another wireless message: "Von Bork missing, believed drowned." And then, "Yacht's lifeboat missing. Several survivors believed landed on East coast."

Mycroft exploded. "Then tell them to send a landing party in pursuit," he cried. "Alert the police in the area, and get them to throw a ring around the landing site."

More uniformed men dashed to and fro. An army sergeant reported this time. "Police in the locality say they will carry out your orders as soon as possible, sir."

"As soon as possible?" bellowed Mycroft. "They will do it immediately. What are they talking about?"

The sergeant stood his ground. "The duty officer for the area said that all his men were out with a Scotland Yard detective investigating a murder, sir. He said he would send a messenger to get them in position for this operation, sir, but it might take an hour or so."

Mycroft could not believe his ears. "A murder!" he exclaimed. "What murder? Where are these men?"

Sherlock Holmes had been leaning over a map. At Mycroft's

question he straightened up and turned to face his brother. "I think you will find they are at a place called Heaven's Portal," he said.

And so they were. It was almost an hour later that the Chief Constable reported his men had thrown a cordon around the spot where Von Bork had landed, for it had indeed been established that he was one of the small group to escape. We knew by then that they had beached their lifeboat near the village, for it had been found by the landing party of warships. A further report made it clear that the Germans had spent about half-an-hour in the village, and a man later identified as Von Bork had been spotted driving a stolen motor car by an unsuspecting police constable not informed of the huge manhunt which was under way. More messages were sent out, but by midnight the vehicle had been found abandoned in the eastern suburbs of London. Von Bork had arrived back in the capital. But this time, he was a free man.

"We can do no more here, Watson," said a weary Sherlock Holmes. "It seems it is once more my task to apprehend this man." He turned to Mycroft. "I am sorry your system failed, brother. But we shall catch him, never fear."

Mycroft looked his younger brother full in the face. "You must, Sherlock," he said. "You must. Von Bork has been held *incommunicado* because of the vital information he possesses. As you are aware, he knows the strength of much of our defences and, before you arrested him, he had learned the identity of one of our most trusted agents, an agent who is at the very centre of the Kaiser's High Command and who keeps us appraised of every policy move they make. You may be aware that at present Germany's armed strength is superior to this country's. That one agent is holding the very balance of power. If we lose that advantage, we will be overrun in weeks, months at the most. Von Bork must be prevented from passing that information to his masters. Now he is back in London you must stop him, Sherlock. Consider every authority at your disposal, but you must catch that man. If you fail, the war is lost."

A Special from Victoria

When I entered our sitting room late the next morning, it was at once evident that Holmes had not retired during the night. As was his wont when a problem of especial difficulty was exercising his mind, he had arranged a pile of cushions, collected from random places in our rooms, on the hearth before the fire, and there he had sat through the night hours. The air was heavy with the reek of tobacco, and I crossed at once to the window and threw it open. As the atmosphere quickly cleared, it revealed the gaunt features of my friend, pipe in mouth, staring at various maps thrown on the floor at his feet.

"Holmes, have you eaten anything this morning? No mind can function at its best without any form of sustenance."

Sherlock Holmes glanced up wearily. "No, Watson; at times like these I find the process of preparing and eating food too distracting. Von Bork is unlikely to be worrying over the state of his stomach at the moment: why, then, should I?" He broke off and beckoned me to him. I settled in my chair.

"Now, be a willing and silent listener for a moment, Watson, while we consider the events of yesterday and await the message which I trust will come, that Von Bork's exact whereabouts have been discovered. We missed him by a few hours yesterday; he and his accomplices were sailing fast down the Thames estuary. When spotted by the ships of the Navy, what would you have done in his place, Watson? Would you not have put in to the nearest sheltered part of the coastline, a mere two or three miles away? The maps I have here," Holmes indicated the profusion of charts before him, "show that this area of Essex by the coast is heavy with marshland, and the coastline itself is rutted with narrow inlets: he could have hidden where he chose and escaped easily under cover of darkness, whatever the strength of our search-parties. Yet what did we see? Our quarry sailed some twelve miles with the Royal Navy in his wake, almost as if he were aiming for that specific village of Heaven's Portal; he seemed deliberately to court danger to reach that little town. Inexplicable, Watson, inexplicable. We seem to be haunted by Heaven's Portal.

"The man is obliged to reach the Kaiser at the earliest possible date; he must have been making for a German vessel stationed off the coast

- he would then be transported at all speed to the nearest safe European haven, there to disembark and proceed to Germany and Berlin. But he has returned to London, instead of biding his time on the Essex coast. And I am fairly certain that I know the reason for his change of plans. The Kaiser is not in Berlin."

I started forward. "How do you know that, Holmes?"

"A telephone call of seeming irrelevance this morning, my dear Watson. You were still slumbering when a man from Mycroft's department informed me that the Kaiser was reported to have left his capital yesterday, intending to inspect his troops at the front: his base will be the château at the village of Lombez. Presumably this piece of information was transmitted by our agent at William's elbow and thus must be believed.

"This, therefore, must have caused Von Bork to change his ultimate destination: with the information he has, it would be entirely pointless to arrive in Berlin if the Kaiser and his staff are in France. Thus, despite the fraught situation in which he found himself last night when we were close on his heels, and having received this same information I know not how, he changed his mind, doubled back on his tracks, and must now be attempting to make his way to the south coast, and thence travel to France. We are indeed pitted against a worthy foe, one who is able to take vital decisions under the most trying of circumstances."

"I take it, Holmes, that a close watch is being kept along the south coast?" I interjected.

Holmes nodded. "Even nearer home than that. Insofar as it is possible, there is a blockade around London, with especial reference to all routes leading south. We shall hope to catch the German in this net; but if he manages to evade us, then rest assured that there are police at every obvious port and, indeed, at certain places not so obvious.

"But I am not happy - I am not convinced that all our efforts will prevent his escape. And so it is that you will see my bag, packed and ready by the door; I should advise you to do the same, Watson. This evening may find us on the other side of the Channel. My reasoning must be correct. Von Bork simply does not have the time to waste laying false trails for us to follow. He must take the simplest and most direct route that will lead him to Kaiser William, and the destruction inevitably resulting upon his arrival of one of this country's most important sources of enemy intelligence. He must go south. He must!"

The telephone rang, shrill and insistent, and Holmes crossed the room in a single cat-like movement. At the same moment there came a loud knock at the door downstairs, and I hastened out of the room.

On the step were Wiggins and two constables. The Scotland Yard man grasped my arm. "A car has broken through one of our barriers at Maidstone; several shots were fired, and a sergeant is badly wounded. One of the men in the car answers to the description of Von Bork!" I hurried back up the stairs, the policemen behind me, to find Holmes at the door of our apartment.

"Ah, Wiggins, a breakdown in your procedure; I would have hoped that your attaining so high a position at Scotland Yard would have obviated the necessity for me to be delayed on the telephone by one of your junior officers, while you yourself are at my threshold. Yes, your man has told me what has occurred, and it is exactly what I foretold would happen ... is that not so, Watson? The man is making for Dover or Folkestone; if the incident had happened further to the west, I might have suspected Southampton, but Maidstone clearly indicates one of the two primary Channel ports. It is a pity that he has already been permitted to go so far," Holmes added, glancing reproachfully at Wiggins, "but that is not to be helped now. Watson, we have reached a crisis. Pack what you can, and come this instant."

Understanding the need for urgency, I hurried to my room, flung a few essentials into my Gladstone, and rejoined the small group in the sitting room. Holmes replaced the telephone earpiece as I entered.

"A special is being engaged for us at Victoria, even at this extreme short notice. It is pointless for us to attempt a chase along the roads: the Germans, assuming it is indeed they, have too much of a lead; but I fancy, if the railway line to Dover can be cleared in front of us as we go, we should be able to arrive a little before them. We are lucky that it is Sunday today: there will be fewer regular trains on the lines to be held up or diverted. Come, all of you!"

In the ten minutes it took for us to reach Victoria, officials at the station had by some miracle been able to prepare a special train for us: an engine, tender and one following carriage. The requisite clearances had been given, and it was not difficult to understand why everything had been carried out with such expedition when we saw the portly figure of Mycroft Holmes standing on the platform, engaging the driver in conversation.

"My dear Mycroft, we seem forever to be meeting at railway stations. How could you know we would be coming here?" cried Holmes.

"Simplicity itself, Sherlock. I received the news of Von Bork and his people at about the same time as you did, and I did not have to wait for my friends to pack their worldly belongings." I suddenly became aware that they were all gazing at me as I desperately stuffed a recalcitrant shirt into my bag. "In any case," continued Mycroft, "without these slight hindrances, my official car was able to convey me here in exactly three and three quarter minutes. There was, of course, no question but that you, Sherlock, would correctly surmise that a special would be needed to stop Von Bork.

"And now, I wish you all luck. Remember, brother, it is essential that the German does not get the ear of the Kaiser. If he manages to cross to France, you must follow him and you must stop him by any means you may think fit?" Mycroft spoke with icy calm and I realised the import of what he said.

"Surely now, Mycroft, you can tell me who our government agent is with the Kaiser? Why all the secrecy?" Holmes queried, climbing into the carriage.

Mycroft shook his head. "Not even at this stage, Sherlock. It is by no means certain that you will need to know the agent's identity; after all, you are unlikely to have to penetrate to the German headquarters yourself. No, better that you should not know, and that you carry out this government business in the dark to that extent. My department operates on the need-to-know principle, and that must apply even to you." Sherlock Holmes half smiled. "Had it been anybody but you, Mycroft, I would drop the case on the instant." The brothers clasped hands, then the driver signalled that all was ready with the engine, and Wiggins and I, accompanied by the two constables, climbed on board. The wheels started turning and in a few minutes we were steaming at high speed through the sleepy suburbs of London, disturbing the Sabbath calm as we sped on our mission to halt the German master spy.

Beneath the White Cliffs

Onwards through southern England we hurtled, always urged on to higher speeds by the signals of clearance that seemed to stretch out for miles before us. The railway authorities had been made fully aware of the importance and gravity of our mission, and not once were we halted. At no stage were we even compelled to slow down.

The outcome of our chase was, of course, to be determined by events yet to happen, and so Holmes did not permit himself, or us, indeed, to dwell on possible results and what might occur later in the day. We allowed his conversation to dominate and were regaled with brilliant discourses on the effect the war was having upon the economy of Brazil, the intrinsic superiority of cats over dogs despite the latters' tracking abilities, the extraordinary batting performances of the cricketer Prince Ranjitsinhji, and certain structural weaknesses in Bede's *Historia Ecclesiastica*. We were as children at his feet and Holmes, sensing his powerful hold, shone magnificently. It was only a hurriedly waved green flag as we approached the outer limits of Dover that brought us back to the realities of the chase. Holmes was not surprised by the incident.

"I spoke briefly to Mycroft before we left Victoria and asked for such a signal to be given if the Germans and their car were still on course for Dover. The rapid waving of the flag, as opposed to its merely being displayed, is also part of the signal: it tells me that our German friends are actually in the town now. We have, of course, Watson, been permitting the fugitives to get thus far unhindered, after the initial breakthrough at Maidstone. I think it is wiser that Wiggins and I should be on hand, rather than leave Von Bork to the tender ministrations of a police or army marksman. And now, gentlemen, I believe we have arrived." As he spoke, we were all thrown forward by the momentum of the engine as it screeched to a halt only a few feet from the buffers which marked the end of the line.

Holmes pressed a coin into the hand of our expert driver and, with a murmured word of thanks, strode across the platform to where a small huddle of uniformed men were waiting. Wiggins and I, happy to place ourselves in the hands of Sherlock Holmes, followed without speaking. A police sergeant broke off what he was saying to Holmes as we approached, and snapped a sharp salute as he recognised Wiggins.

"Pardon, sir, I thought there was only going to be Mr. Holmes here, sir." He looked uncomfortably at his superior.

"There is no need to worry, sergeant," said Wiggins. "Pray continue what you were telling Mr. Holmes."

"Well, sir, it's as this way. We let the car through into the town without apprehending it, as we was ordered to by London..." He looked at Wiggins, as if seeking confirmation, then continued. "It's a large Daimler they're in, and it is the man we're looking for, sir - that's been checked by an officer who's seconded here at the moment from London, sir."

"Inspector Mansfield?" queried Wiggins. The sergeant nodded in affirmation, then Holmes broke in impatiently.

"And while we stand here discussing that situation, an entirely new one may now exist. Where are the men at this moment, sergeant? Are they near the docks?"

"No, sir; my last report by telephone, not five minutes ago from officers who are following them, said that they were now relaxing a little and were driving slowly around the centre of Dover, presumably so as not to give any idea that they was in a hurry, sir. I think as how we've fooled them, sir."

"Possibly in the short term, but they must know that the hue-and-cry will have been raised after they shot that policeman at the roadblock, and they really cannot afford to lose much time. I think, Wiggins, that we should proceed to the centre of the town and beard these villains without more delay. Their exact position, sergeant?"

"Last report, they was driving between the High Street and Maison Dieu Road, sir - a quarter of a mile from the Priory station here."

"Then let's be gone, gentlemen," and so saying, Holmes headed towards the station exit.

Two cars were waiting for us in the forecourt and, in a moment, we were driving quickly into the centre of Dover. At a road junction, we swept round to the left, and found ourselves confronted by long columns of soldiers marching towards us. Wiggins cursed bitterly and looked fleetingly at Holmes. My friend stared straight ahead, saying nothing.

"We'll have to give way to them, sir," said Wiggins.

"It's the weekly convoy, sir, from Dover over to France," chimed in the local sergeant. By now, our cars had been forced to a halt, and the serried ranks of British soldiers marched past, perfectly drilled; they might almost have been back on their Aldershot parade ground. My heart swelled with pride as I saw the valiant way in which these young men were facing their appalling destiny their heads held rigidly high, their eyes looking neither to right nor left. We were almost the only onlookers, for the townspeople of Dover had long ago become accustomed to such sights and they continued upon their usual daily business with little thought, I fancy, of the dangers these men might have to face in a few short hours over in France.

My reflections were interrupted when a police officer appeared on the other side of the road, waving frantically at us. I drew Holmes's attention to the man and, as Wiggins was about to leave the car, the constable began to make his way across the road, slipping through the ranks of soldiers.

"The Daimler's turned out of Maison Dieu Road, sir," cried the man as he reached us. "It looks as if it's going down to the docks along Marine Parade."

"Then that, too, is our destination," commented Holmes drily, and our driver needed no second exhortation to pull the car out of its position at the kerb and to turn parallel to the marching regiment. Almost on two wheels, we careered around a corner and forced a passage through the traffic down towards the sea.

"The thrill of the chase, eh, Watson?" said Holmes quizzically. "Quite like old times. It reminds me of the evening we spent on the Thames back in the eighties, when our quarry was perhaps less important but quite as dangerous." As our car accelerated along the sea-front, I well remembered the excitement of that night, so many years before, when Holmes and I had pursued the launch *Aurora* and its cargo of Jonathan Small and the vicious Andaman Islander, Tonga.

A seagull flew low across the path of our car and the driver swore angrily as he swerved to avoid it. Above us, as we sped along, the great white cliffs stood out in bold relief, the cold sunlight etching deep shadows among the crags. As I looked up, shading my eyes against the glare of the sky, I could make out the small forms of people out walking, enjoying a day by the sea, and wholly unaware of the vital drama being played a few hundred feet below them.

With a sharp cry, Wiggins pointed ahead, then crouched down below the level of the windscreen of the car. I snatched a glance towards the rapidly-approaching port buildings, and saw what had attracted the detective's attention. A large black car was slewed round at the main entrance gate, and while several men were climbing out and disappearing into the gloom inside, one thick-set character had turned and was resting his hand upon the smooth Daimler bonnet. In his grasp I could see the tell-tale glint of grey metal that meant a revolver was aimed in our direction, and, as a reflex action, I pulled Holmes by the shoulder and forced him to protect himself. He had, I think, failed to notice the danger. A dull report echoed and of a sudden our car careered in an arc to the right, then came to a faltering halt, our driver bent low over his wheel. I would have stopped to tend the injured man, but by now Sherlock Holmes was galvanised into action.

"No, Watson, no time for that! The man's dead: can you not see the blood on his head? Keep low beneath the car!" So saying, he loosed off a single shot, which brought quick reply, one bullet striking the hub of a wheel uncomfortably close to my head. My military eye told me in an instant that ours was an untenable position. Our car had been forced to halt perhaps eighty paces from the embarkation buildings, completely unprotected on either side. The following car, containing three local police officers, was in a similar predicament, and not one of those men had the consolation of being armed. I glanced quickly around and saw one man spin and fall backwards, throwing his hands to his face as a bullet struck his temple. Beside me, Holmes was silent, staring at our solitary adversary.

"One man, Watson, and he is permitting his comrades to escape! He must be disposed of if we are to capture Von Bork."

"Look over there, sir, to the right beyond the short jetty. A launch is setting out!" cried Wiggins, and indeed I then saw the snub nose of a grey naval launch slowly gathering speed through the calm water, its prow towards the open sea. "My God, they're escaping; they're out of our hands!" cried the wiry professional, and as he spoke, he stood up to his full height; seemingly unaware of any danger, he fired three shots towards the single German who kept us at bay. Abruptly the man disappeared, and I heard a faint clatter of metal. Sherlock Holmes lunged forward eagerly.

"You have got him, Wiggins!"

By this time, the columns of soldiers which had been marching through the town had reached our battleground, and their commanding officer, having accurately sized up the situation, had acted quickly in deploying his men so that they were able to cover Holmes, Wiggins and myself as we ran, as fast as our tired legs would carry us, towards our quarry. I have had the same sensations when charging the Ghazis at Maiwand. There was no fire directed at us and as we rounded the car, I saw our adversary leaning against the running board, clasping his stomach and breathing heavily. Slowly he slid forward as we reached him, his left arm shooting straight out before him, as if in some muscular spasm.

In a moment, Holmes was kneeling by the man's side. "Von Bork: *wohin geht er*?" The German words came naturally from his tongue. The dying man looked up in some bewilderment, then shook his head and gazed vacantly around. Holmes shook him, speaking this time in English, and in a somewhat more brutal fashion.

"You are dying, man, and if you do not bleed to death here, you will assuredly be shot for spying. You have nothing to gain by silence and can only help yourself by giving us the information we need. Where is Von Bork, your master, going? What is his destination?" Holmes accentuated each word of his questioning with a shake of the man's body that could only have brought intense pain and suffering. I should, perhaps, have intervened, but such matters of state were involved, and so much hung on the answers the wounded German might give, that I held back and said nothing. A group of soldiers had gathered round the fallen man by this time, and all about him his frightened eyes could only have seen levelled weapons and imminent retribution. His gaze wandered back to Holmes's face, and it was clear that he had resigned himself to his fate. Weakly he shrugged his shoulders.

"They go ... they are travelling in ... Paris."

Holmes looked sharply across to me, then back down at the German. "Why does Von Bork go to Paris?" he asked urgently. There was a long silence. The harsh call of a gull wheeling above the scene of drama broke the hush and the German, as if moved to speak further by the sound of the sea-bird, beckoned Holmes to bend down closer to him; indeed, I could scarcely hear his words when they came.

"He gives ... information ... *zu Herr Lubin* ... Paris!" Then there was a rush of blood from his mouth and he slumped forward, chin resting upon his spattered jacket.

Holmes looked up. "So, Von Bork goes to France, and to Paris. We have no chance now to stop his little craft from reaching France, thus we must follow and meet him in Paris." He broke off and gazed bleakly out to sea. "Herr Lubin must be the prime German agent in Paris, and Von Bork will be giving his information to him; if he cannot get word directly to the Kaiser, his next course of action must be to give the details to one who presumably has well-oiled lines of communication behind the Allied trenches. Our duty is clear." From an inside pocket of his cape, Holmes took a pencil and notebook and scrawled a few words down. "Here, Wiggins, transmit that message to my brother Mycroft in London and see that the necessary formalities are taken care of Watson and I must travel to France today and be in Paris by nightfall, if at all possible. There is no time to apply through the regular channels for permission to cross to the Continent, and so we must take responsibility for our actions upon ourselves." An elderly gentleman in dark blue uniform spoke at this moment. "I am the harbour-master, sir. I understand that your business is of the gravest urgency, and so shall order a small steam craft for your passage now. It will be ready in a matter of minutes, Mr. Holmes." He turned and moved off at some speed toward the embarkation sheds.

Gradually, the group of interested onlookers drifted away, as the army formations were regrouped and the local police gathered to discuss and report on the morning's adventurous happenings. Only Wiggins and I were left with Holmes, together with the body of our German informant. Holmes smiled up at me. "Mycroft never spoke a truer word than when he said 'I hear of Sherlock everywhere.' I fear, Watson, that when the harbour-master at Dover recognises me and knows my name, your lurid renderings of our small adventures have gone too far in the process of popular deification. Let us hope that any readers you may have in Paris are not so instantly aware of my identity." He chuckled drily as he walked off towards a distant jetty.

An Eventful Crossing

As the harbour-master had promised, a small launch was made ready for us within a quarter of an hour. He accompanied Wiggins and I down to the small jetty at a distant end of Dover harbour, where Holmes had already been waiting impatiently for some minutes. As the men untied and threw off connecting ropes from two bollards, Holmes and the Scotland Yard man shook hands warmly.

"I only wish I could come with you and the doctor, sir," said Wiggins fervently.

Holmes smiled. "I fear your superiors might have something to say on that score, inspector. No, whatever attractions this chase has for you, it would take you into areas wherein your authority as a member of His Majesty's Metropolitan Police Force would be as nothing. Even Watson and I are likely to get ourselves into complexities that will need the combined powers of the British and French civil services - not to mention their armies - to extricate us. I hope we shall meet again safely, Wiggins." A shadow passed suddenly over his brow. "It will take more than the machine-guns of the Western Front to keep me from my bees and my little cottage on the Downs. And besides, we must return for the Albert Hall concert on the last day of the year. Now, Watson, we must start, and keep these sailors waiting no longer, not to speak of Von Bork losing himself in France before we have the opportunity to pick up his trail."

I passed a few final words with Wiggins as Holmes swung himself down onto the deck of our craft, then clambered down the narrow steps myself and helped one of our crew members take our sparse luggage below. Wiggins waved farewell, the harbour-master saluted, and with a snort of smoke from the stumpy stack, we moved away from the jetty and pointed our prow towards France.

It was an eventful crossing. A sharp wind whipped around our ears whenever we stood on deck, and for the most part, only the hapless junior officer who was steering had to remain above to brave the elements. Sherlock Holmes and I stayed below, making ourselves as comfortable as we could against the cold, and fortified in our attempts to do so by a few nips from the brandy bottle which the harbour-master had thoughtfully pressed into my hands. Hunched in a corner of the small cabin, his soft hat pressed down on his forehead by the low ceiling and his overcoat draped haphazardly over his shoulders, my companion seemed disconsolate, but the constant spirals of smoke from his pipe, and the look of sharp concentration on his lean features, told my practised eye that Holmes was far from dispirited.

I broke the silence. "Well, Holmes, what are our plans on arrival at Calais? Do we travel on to Paris immediately?"

"All haste to the capital, yes, Watson," rejoined Holmes, "always with the proviso that Von Bork will also be making his way there as quickly as possible. I have already indicated that it is in his and the Kaiser's interests that the German agent in Paris should have full details of the case as soon as may be. There are one or two addresses in Paris I know of where Herr Lubin might be found and whither Von Bork must be heading. They are, however, based on information the government had at the beginning of last month, and so may not be entirely accurate now. One of those addresses will be an early port of call; if that fails, then we visit another and so on. I shall also instruct the Prefect of Police, a gentleman I happen to know to give us any aid we may require. There is, if I recall aright, a hotel of the first order in the rue de Rivoli which will afford us a central location and base for our operations. The Hotel Wagram. I remember it well when I was able to be of service in apprehending Huret, the boulevard assassin."

I interposed. "Holmes, the expense will surely be more than you and I can bear? For myself, I have only a few pounds - there was no time to take any more when we left Baker Street."

Holmes waved his hand airily, dismissing my objection. "It would be surly indeed if Monsieur Dalmy charged you and I the fourteen franc pension rate. I fancy that if I remind him of the Clichy butcher and his extraordinary birdcage the manager will be more than willing to let us bed down gratis."

"Holmes, really!" I expostulated. "It is not typical of you to take advantage of any information you might have to blackmail people who may be of use to you."

Holmes chuckled. "Indeed, Watson, it would be atypical of me ... if I were doing it. But Monsieur Dalmy once found himself in a somewhat parlous position in the Latin Quarter, and he will be only too glad to recall how I was able to assist him. No, we shall have no worries on the score of expense."

Suddenly there came an excited cry from above. Holmes and I rose up as one and swung open the small door that led on to the deck. The man at the wheel was pointing ahead.

"D'you see her, sir? We have the advantage on her!" I peered into the darkness, and at first could see nothing. But, as my eyes became accustomed to the gloom, I thought I could make out the distant shape of a small boat similar to ours, tossing on the waves. Holmes shaded his eyes.

"Can it be them, Holmes?" I queried. "They had a good half-hour's start on us." My friend said nothing, but stared keenly at the far off craft.

"Yes, it is," he announced eventually, with an air of finality. "I recognise the orange slash of colour around the stern. They must have encountered some problems. Nevertheless, they are still a goodly distance in front of us, and I should not be sanguine about catching them." He turned to the captain of our boat. "However, make all speed, my man. It would save us a deal of trouble if we were able to apprehend the villains here."

The sailor signalled his assent and, opening the speaking tube, called down to the furnace-men below. "More steam there, men; full speed ordered!" It was remarkable how the small launch accelerated beneath our feet, as a runner might do as he rounds the final bend and sees the tape before him and a record to beat. But almost at the same time as our surge of power, the ever-present wind roared even more fiercely, and with it came a few drops of icy rain.

A sailor came from below with two pairs of oilskins, and by the time Holmes and I had donned them, the rain was slanting down across our faces, searing our skins. Gradually, in our efforts to control our own course, we became less and less aware of the German boat ahead, and after about twenty minutes it had disappeared from sight. The sailors cursed bitterly, but Holmes did not seem disturbed. He merely shrugged his shoulders, threw a half-smile in my direction, and went down below. I stayed up on deck for a few minutes more, straining my eyes against the darkness and hail, searching out the tell-tale band of orange that would identify our prey. But eventually I was compelled to give up, and I joined my friend in the cabin.

"We wait, my dear Watson," said Holmes, clutching the table as the boat gave a particularly violent heave.

And so passed the remainder of our four-and-a half hour crossing. I suppose I must have fallen into a doze, since when Holmes laid his hand on my shoulder to tell me of our arrival on foreign soil, for an instant I did not know where we were.

"Calais, Watson: the starting point for so many English adventurers, from Edward the Third to our poor selves."

When we climbed up on deck, I saw for myself the immense expertise with which our captain had navigated the boat into Calais harbour. In the appalling winter conditions, he had steered firm and true down the narrow entry into what I knew to be the Avant-Port, and negotiated a difficult right turn into the Port d'Échouage, by which was the station. We only had time for hurried thanks and farewells before a rope ladder was thrown down from the jetty above and we clambered unsteadily up onto dry land. As I regained my footing and accustomed myself to a surface that did not rock beneath my feet, Sherlock Holmes gestured further on down the jetty. There, riding up and down on the waves, was a small steam vessel such as ours had been, but with one difference: a broad orange line was painted around its stern.

On to Paris

As I followed Sherlock Holmes, a small, portly figure detached itself from the surrounding gloom. He came towards us, hands outstretched.

"*Messieurs, messieurs!*" he cried and, reaching Holmes, began to talk volubly to him in French. From his blue uniform and cap, together with the short revolver at his belt, I took him to be a gendarme.

"Watson, it goes against my nature to do this, but extreme circumstances demand extreme measures. Have you a sovereign about you? This French official is choosing to be obstructive and only cash will soothe him. He wishes to see all sorts of documents and papers of entry that we had neither time nor opportunity to obtain in England."

"Bribing an official, Holmes?" I asked.

He shrugged. "Extreme circumstances," he replied. I shuffled through my pocket and produced the desired gold piece. The effect on the French policeman was instantaneous. His face creased into an outsize grin and his gestures became even more expansive as he showed his thanks. Holmes entered into further conversation with the man, asking questions in a peculiar argot that I could not understand. Finally, it seemed that both parties were satisfied and, with further protestations of gratitude, the little gendarme went back into the shadows whence he had emerged.

"A man from the Carcassonne area; they have a singular style of speech in those parts. Indeed, some years ago, I carried out some research into possible links between French dialects and the language in certain Islamic holy writings.

"However, with the aid of your money - refundable in full by brother Mycroft, I assure you - I have elicited from our uniformed friend that no party has gone into the station these last three hours, and Von Bork and his companions can only have reached Calais half an hour at the most before us. Therefore they are taking some alternative form of transport to Paris. What time is it, Watson?"

I dragged out my watch. "Late, Holmes, it's approaching eleven o'clock."

Holmes paused a moment, his pensive face etched sharply against a momentary flash of light from the station building that loomed beside us. "I think it must still be rail travel for us. There is a late civilian train in a few minutes, I am informed. With luck, we should arrive at the Gare du Nord at five tomorrow, thence quickly to the Wagram and on to the first of my addresses in central Paris where our friend Herr Lubin, Von Bork's contact, may be hiding. Hurry aboard!''

"Are there no customs facilities, Holmes?" I queried as we walked quickly towards a ticket booth.

My companion looked back at me over his shoulder. "We have only sparse luggage, Watson, and neither of us carry any contraband. Besides in wartime, regulations without which peace would be intolerable often tend to go by the board. On arrival in Paris, they may perhaps wish to search our baggage, in which case speed will have to be purchased by yet more coins of the realm."

Holmes was able to exchange one of the aforesaid coins for two tickets and some small change and, with seconds to spare, we swung on to the Paris train. We were the only passengers in our compartment, and with this I was happy enough in that I could stretch out my weary body. I deposited my bag in the rack above our heads and settled in a corner seat. As the train drew out of the station, I was vaguely aware of the formless darkened centre of Calais through the carriage window, before I drifted off into a deep sleep.

At one point, I recall being aware of some movement in our compartment; Holmes was, I remember, standing at the window, fingering the strap. But the exertions of the previous day had been too much for me and unconsciousness swept over me once more.

It was only when a hand grasped me firmly by the shoulder and shook it that I became fully awake. A bright light arched into the carriage from outside and a great belching of steam, together with the multitude of cries from newspaper-vendors, platform attendants and stallholders told me that we had arrived at our destination.

"Three hours late, Watson, " said Sherlock Holmes bitterly. "It is now eight o'clock. A troop train running before us on the line outside Amiens broke down, and we were obliged to cool our heels for three hours. I think you half awoke while I was expressing some little impatience. The upshot is, Watson, that Von Bork has almost certainly reached Paris before us and has been able to alert Lubin as to the identity of our man in the Kaiser's camp. By the deuce, if we are thwarted because of a rail accident..." He left the sentence unfinished.

It was the work of a moment to collect our belongings and extricate ourselves from the train carriage. We crossed the wide causeway of the station and passed out into the sunshine of the forecourt. Here a collection of conveyances awaited passengers such as ourselves, though not so many, I might add, as there would have been in habitual peacetime circumstances. Out of the choice of horse-drawn cabs, motorised cabs and taxi-meter cabs, Holmes selected one of the last-named. The driver handed over his number to Holmes, an action which perplexed me until my friend later told me that it was to obviate the necessity for any disagreement, should a passenger have cause for complaint against a cabby. Then the cab took its place in the front row reserved for engaged vehicles, and while a minor official checked our bags, I availed myself of the opportunity to purchase a morning newspaper. Then Holmes and I climbed into the cab, the driver set his meter, Holmes called out the name of the hotel that was to be our destination, and we rattled off.

As we proceeded on our way, I could not help but remark to Holmes how unlike a city at war Paris seemed to be. Only a few weeks previously, the advancing German armies had been within ten miles of the Parisian outskirts, a hostile proximity which had led to the celebrated rush of buses and cabs from the city with reinforcements to bolster the defensive lines. But that might have been a year since, for all the obvious signs of beleaguerment or shortage. In the crisp winter sunlight, Paris was as alive as ever it might have been before the European catastrophe: roadside cafes seemed to ply their trade as always; the streets were full of traffic, even at this comparatively early hour, as sedate businessmen went to their offices; the pavements of the rue Lafayette seemed almost impassable with the throng of clerks going to work for those businessmen, highly fashionable ladies of all ages perambulating and gazing in well-stocked shop windows, and the habitual paraphernalia of flower-sellers, errand boys and mendicants. But then my companion pointed out several groups of uniformed officers, clearly on leave, but nonetheless with the wary look of those who had seen action not long before. At one point, as our cab negotiated the interchange of streets behind the Place de l'Opéra, vehicles travelling in the same direction as ourselves had to pause for some minutes as a column of men marched towards the Gare de l'Est, a station close to that whence we had just come, but serving points away from the northern coast and so, I surmised, used for the ferrying of troops to the trenches.

Because of the night-time delay, and the consequent damage to our chances of catching our quarry, Holmes remained passive throughout our journey, commenting only once on the æsthetic incompatibility of the white dome of the church of the Sacré Cœur seen in the distance behind us over the grimy exterior of a department store. Everything about the man denoted a suppressed tension, with none of the obvious vibrancy that would have been apparent had the case been going our way. Only when the cab debouched out of the Avenue de l'Opéra and turned left into the rue de Rivoli did he rouse himself from his torpor and show any real interest in the proceedings.

As the cab drew up outside two elaborately carved doors, with the words *Hotel Wagram* ingeniously cut into the panelling, Holmes sprang out and, glancing cursorily at the meter, held out some coins to the driver. We collected the two bags and a commissionaire stepped quickly forward.

"Now be a good fellow and order a cold lunch at one, will you, Watson?" said my friend. "I'm off on business with which you cannot help at the moment." Presumably he perceived the look of hurt and annoyance on my face, for he added, "My goodness, Watson, do you think I should not have you by me if I were in danger, or if the case were to reach its dénouement? No, my dear friend, never could a man have a more trusty companion than yourself in troubled times. Rest assured that there will be action enough in the near future that will satisfy even your veteran appetite. Mention my name to Monsieur Dalmy, and if that does not instantly procure you the best breakfast in Paris, then I am no judge of character. Install yourself and our luggage in a room and await my return." Sherlock Holmes moved away down the street, but turned just before he was lost in the crowd. "A cold meat salad for preference, Watson, and make sure that your revolver is loaded." With those enigmatic words he disappeared.

Somewhat shaken by the unexpected turn of events, but heartened by Holmes's confidence in me, and certain that he would not embark on any vital part of the investigation without me on hand, I did as he had instructed and was soon enjoying a superb meal, provided by an ebullient Monsieur Dalmy.

"*Un intime de Monsieur Sherlock Holmes,*" he had said upon my identifying myself, "*mais, c'est formidable, c'est justement magnifique...*" and he had proceeded to lecture me on the events many years before which had led to Holmes and him meeting, events of which Holmes had already given me some indication. It certainly appeared that the man had every cause to be in debt to my friend, and I gathered that, as Holmes had foretold, the question of payment for anything that his establishment had to offer would be taken as the grossest discourtesy. I was happy, I explained in broken French, to avail myself of his hospitality and beautiful hotel.

For all that, I was very careful, on reaching our room and locking the door, to make sure the chambers of my revolver were all loaded.

The Latin Quarter

It was not until nearly lunchtime that Holmes returned. In the meantime, I busied myself about our hotel room, with my mind occupied for the most part in working out how we could find Von Bork. He was one man, lost among thousands in the French capital, and it was of the most vital importance that he was captured quickly. And yet, I mused, surely he would be able to hide himself with the greatest of ease, and contact the mysterious Herr Lubin at any time convenient to himself. To counter him, we had Sherlock Holmes and myself, doughty enough when a baronet is murdered in Hampshire, with the clues there to be discovered; but engaged on a chase in war-torn Paris for a man who would stop at nothing to ensure our destruction if we were ever lucky enough to track him down - that was quite a different tale. Turning these facts dully over in my mind led only to a feeling of annoyance at our impending failure, and a twinge of pain in my shoulder where a Jezail bullet had penetrated many years before. In desperation I snatched up a cheap novel which I had hurriedly taken from our Baker Street lodgings upon the previous day, and attempted to involve myself in the petty fictitious mystery.

A knock sounded urgently at the door and, keeping my revolver handy, although hidden, I called on the unknown to enter. The door slowly swung open and a brass trolley, loaded with cold meats and salads, preceded the form of a waiter into the room.

"Where to put, sir?" the man asked in appalling English, bending low over a particular platter as he tossed the salad. Absent-mindedly I indicated a far corner of the room and returned to my book. I heard the metallic whine of the trolley-wheels, then a flash of white caught my attention on the instant, and I drew out my Webley from behind the ink-well on the desk at which I was sitting.

"Quite fast, Watson, but not, I fancy, fast enough!" came the dry chuckling tones of a familiar voice. I looked up in astonishment. Sherlock Holmes was standing carelessly in the alcove, a white waiter's coat slung over his arm. He smiled when he saw my face and the discomposure that must have been registered thereon.

"Sorry, Watson. You know I can never resist a touch of the theatrical. The true servant was just readying himself to knock at the door when I appeared, and it was the work of a few seconds aided by the modest expenditure of a franc, to transform myself by means of this coat."

"Holmes," I cried, "I am amazed that you are in humour enough for pranks of this nature. Where have you been?"

Holmes had been fastidiously arranging a portion of beef on a slice of bread while I spoke, and he took a sizeable bite before he answered me. "I am in such humour, dear friend, because I can afford to be. Von Bork is not yet in Paris."

His words had the desired effect on me; I sat bolt upright in my seat. "You mean that the delay on our train did not permit him to reach here several hours before ourselves? Why, that is excellent news, Holmes. Surely it makes our task easier?"

Holmes nodded his assent. "As you so perceptively say, it does indeed make things easier, although we are talking in relative terms. You may recall that, a moment before we left Dover, I ordered a message to be sent to my brother Mycroft, asking him to see to all the necessary arrangements in view of the short notice under which we were obliged to take our trip. Well, Mycroft seems to have acted with more expedition and fraternal feeling than I would have given him credit for. Doubtless it is the somewhat frenetic atmosphere in the Diogenes war-room that causes it. Be that as it may," Holmes continued, wagging a finger at me as I showed some impatience, "I have communicated this morning with Sir Francis Bertie, who is His Majesty's Ambassador here, only to find out that his staff received a message by Morse code late last night to the effect that Von Bork was making his way here, that we were not far behind and that, if seen, he should be watched closely but not apprehended. The information, together with a detailed description, was handed on to the Prefect of Police, and so that saved me an extra meeting. Sir Francis was courtesy itself, and has extended to us the full resources at his disposal."

By this time I had begun to feel somewhat hungry in my turn, and I joined Holmes at the trolley, both of us eating directly from it rather than transferring to a table. "There can be no danger, Holmes," I began, "that you have been wrong all along and that Von Bork does not intend to come to Paris at all? I must confess myself still at a loss to understand our good fortune at his not yet arriving, and so am inclined to take the pessimistic view."

My friend shook his head emphatically. "Quite right to be a pessimist, Watson; such a course makes life considerably easier in the long run. But you heard the dying words of that German we left lying on the cold stone of Dover harbour. '*Zu Paris* ... to Herr Lubin,' or words to that effect, and that is surely clear enough. Ever since I heard it, that name has been bothering me. I was sure that I had met it before, and it was not until I was examining some frankly horrifying clothing in a Parisian shop specialising in American imported goods that I re-called where I had seen it. Only eight or nine months ago, while in my guise as the American Altamont, dedicated to the capture of Von Bork in England, I glimpsed once the signatory name on a telegram the German spy received from Paris. To allay suspicion, these telegrams were always in English, and the name at the end of the message was 'Wolf.' Code, of course, but of an elementary nature. The word for 'wolf' in French is *loup,* and if you say the word aloud, Watson, I fancy you will see the link with our friend Herr Lubin.

"Besides, Von Bork is obliged to travel here, rather than go to the Kaiser in person. He has been based in England for two years and then incarcerated in that safest of prisons, the Tower of London." He paused for a moment, and the sneer in his voice told me that Holmes had not yet forgotten Colonel MacWyre's failure of but two days previously. "He is in no position to know the movements of the Kaiser, other than he has left Berlin, or the whereabouts of the German High Command. Added to which, of course, is the fact that, now that they are engaged in war, the Germans have built up a highly efficient and well-organised network of agents throughout Europe. Von Bork, however important his news is, simply cannot break into the circuit to suit himself. Their motto, no doubt, is 'Speed, but orderly speed'; he must go through the correct channels.

"So, all stations are being watched, as are all main road arteries into Paris. I might add, Watson, that we ourselves did not evade the keen watchers at the Gare du Nord this morning. Sir Francis had already been told of our arrival and I was greeted with a glass of immaculate Bollinger '08. Remarkable, is it not, how even in straitened circumstances such as now exist, our embassies around the world are still able to operate in their time-honoured style. And now, Watson, have you sated your hunger? Time for us to leave." Holmes suited action to his words, rising and putting on his coat.

"Where to, Holmes?" I queried, brushing some lingering crumbs from my waistcoat.

Holmes was already at the door of our room. "A digestive walk through the Paris sunshine, taking in the delights afforded by this greatest of European capitals, then by way of the Île de la Cîté and the Préfecture de Police, over the river and into that most secretive part of Paris, the Latin Quarter. The two addresses I have which German agents have been known to use are both in that area and, I am informed, both still in use. It is my conjecture that as soon as our friend Von Bork arrives in Paris, he will make his way to Number Seven, rue Valette. It was there that French police narrowly failed to detain a man simitar in description to our German acquaintance who died in Dover yesterday, only a month ago."

Sherlock Holmes continued to discourse as we stepped out of the Hotel Wagram and turned left down the broad and magnificent rue de Rivoli.

"Should we be lucky enough to find Herr Lubin in residence, then our task will be that much the easier. We shall incapacitate him and then we shall await the arrival of Von Bork. I fancy he will get more than he bargained for when he engineered his escape from the Tower," he added, eyes glinting fiercely.

And so we continued on our way, walking at a reasonable pace yet able to enjoy the winter beauties of the city to which our adventure had brought us. The grey bulk of the Louvre Museum loomed up on our right, then fell away behind us, giving way to a further row of expensive shops. In front of us and to our right could occasionally be seen the tops of the twin towers on the great cathedral of Nôtre Dame, situated on the very island that we were to cross in order to attain the Left Bank of the Seine. At an intersection of roads, I paused for a moment to gaze at an approaching column of marching men, officers gaudily - as I thought - bedecked, in glittering epaulettes and sashes, their men staring resolutely ahead. A number of light artillery pieces brought up the rear; and at this point, my attention was drawn to someone who was clearly a casualty of the front, who stood to attention in the gutter in front of Holmes and myself and saluted the passing soldiers. His military bearing alone would have told me that he was a war veteran, but as he turned, he almost collided with my companion and I saw the glint of the raw sun on a line of medals on his chest. With a muttered apology to Holmes, the man, clearly down on his luck, was soon lost in the crowd that surged across the road after the passage of the troops. I turned to Holmes to make some comment and to my surprise noticed that he was reading a message on a scrap of paper.

"Where on earth did you get that, Holmes?" I asked.

Holmes glanced at me in blank astonishment for a moment. "Can it be that you did not notice that old soldier, Watson? He is, in fact, Guillaume Lamartine Palmier, one of France's most trusted and successful agents, and the note he handed me is from the Prefect of Police. Von Bork has entered Paris from the west; a gendarme reported him an hour since in a coupé. Come, we must call on the gentlemen in the Prefecture, then make all haste to the Latin Quarter and the rue Valette in particular." He quickened his pace and I struggled to keep up with him.

In a few moments, we turned to our right and crossed a portion of the river onto the Île de la Cité. We came out into the great open square before the cathedral, and here Holmes stopped me. "You rest here an instant, Watson. This is the Préfecture de Police here," indicating a gaunt grey building rearing up beside us, "and you are not immediately known within its doors, as I am. If he has not already done so, I must ask the Prefect to set in motion a plan for the capture of Von Bork and Herr Lubin." And with that, he disappeared beneath a great archway.

I amused myself for some minutes, wondering at the magnificence of Nôtre Dame, while at the same time running over in my mind the events that were likely to take place within a short while. Could the two German spies have already met? And if so, might the information Von Bork held, information vital to the success of the Allies, already have been passed on to the German High Command by means of radio?

A sharp tug at my sleeve brought me out of my ruminations and I was confronted by Holmes and a small, self-important individual who nevertheless had the steely look of a true professional in his eyes. The short grizzled man was briefly introduced to me as Henri La Fallière, Prefect of Police. He indicated a motor which had drawn up beside us, and the three of us climbed in and sped away. As we did so, I looked over my shoulder through the rear window of the automobile. Three police vehicles were following close behind us. The traffic in front swept respectfully aside as we proceeded over the connecting bridge and onto the Left Bank of the Seine. As we flashed past, I perceived the familiar artists and booksellers, who attempted to sell their wares along the river's edge glance up to see what caused the flurry of vehicles, then back down to their task, whether of creation or vending. A broken-down cab blocked our passage into the wide Boulevard St Germain; Holmes cursed impatiently, but the obstruction was cleared within a minute and we continued on our way, over the broad thoroughfare and into the network of dusty, narrow streets frequented primarily by students, known the world over as the Latin Quarter.

We drew to a halt before a vast edifice and the Prefect was out of our conveyance immediately, issuing sharp instructions to the men following. The gendarmes - I counted thirteen of them - split up and moved off in various directions. Holmes exchanged a few words with La Fallière, then turned to me.

"This, Watson, is the Sorbonne. Beyond it, a few hundred yards or so, is the rue Valette. One of La Fallière's men has already ensconced himself in a bakery opposite Number Seven, and these others are taking up positions around the house. Of course we have stopped here so as not to give the game away to anyone who may be in the house. Stick close to me, my dear Watson: I feel the dénouement to the case is at hand."

As we followed in the footsteps of the gendarmes, I could not help but feel that now success was bound to attend our cause; inexorably the trap was closing in on Von Bork.

No. 7, rue Valette

The rue Valette was a somewhat unusual street. Opposite the end by which we entered was the imposing structure of the Panthéon. I could not help but mention to Holmes in an undertone that Paris seemed to have more grandiose buildings per square yard even than London. The left-hand side was occupied by the rear of a portion of the University buildings, saving only a short terrace at the further end. Upon the right was a mixture of shop fronts and residential houses of a lower kind. A sudden darkening of the sky and the arrival of a few snowflakes only reinforced the impression of a street that had, perhaps, seen better times, but had now turned on a downward path despite its illustrious surroundings. How sensible of the German spies, I thought, to have established themselves here, in an area not often frequented by police except on the occasion of drunken student disturbances, in a quarter of the city where strange occurrences might be expected to take place and so would not be especially remarked upon.

The flurries of snow became heavier as Holmes, the Prefect and I strode up the street. I drew my coat closer around my shoulders. When we had passed the University buildings, La Fallière indicated noiselessly that we were to follow him across the road onto the other side. We did as he asked, and turned into the narrow doorway of a bakery, the same building, I assumed, as that in which a watching gendarme had been installed. And indeed it was so. We climbed some rickety stairs and emerged into a dusty room, empty save for an ancient chair and a foul smelling pile of rotting clothes thrust into a corner. The policeman, who had settled into the chair, sprang up on our entry to salute the Prefect.

"Well, what news, my man?" asked the senior officer.

"There has been activity in the front room on the upper floor," replied the gendarme, "but I have not been able to make out who is in the building. Perhaps you would like to look yourself, sir?" He handed the Prefect a pair of spy-glasses. We followed La Fallière to the window, shaded on one side by the tattered remnants of a once fine set of curtains. La Fallière leaned on the sill and peered for a few seconds through the glasses. He straightened and turned to Holmes.

"This snow could not have come at a worse moment, Monsieur Holmes. It impedes the view most badly. As the officer says, there is something going on in the front room, but who or what is there, I cannot tell. Previous investigation of the building, conducted under cover of night, when we were sure that it was unoccupied, revealed that the room in question is ... how do you say? ... a room for existence, but nothing of special interest therein. "

"A living-room - quite so," remarked Holmes tersely. "May I?" and he held out his hand for the binoculars. "As you say, the falling snow does tend somewhat to block our view of events; and yet, in another sense, I might have hoped that it would have fallen earlier: there might have been some slight indication of who was in that room if I had been able to examine some prints. But what's this?" Holmes leaned forward suddenly, screwing his eyes up as he strained to see through the glasses.

"What is happening, Holmes?" I said, and that very instant a sharp crack sounded from outside in the street. Sherlock Holmes turned away from the window, his face drained of all its colour.

"La Fallière, one of your men has taken a shot at Von Bork!"

"Nom de Dieu!" exploded the Prefect.

Holmes dashed for the door. "Come, Watson, no time to lose! Draw your revolver!" As his footsteps clattered down the bare wooden stairs, I unceremoniously pushed the Prefect aside and followed. Here at last was the action we had been waiting for, after the long hours of tedium on the train and in the hotel; and in this crisis I was immediately aware that Holmes and I would be of more importance by far than Monsieur La Fallière and his entire force of Parisian gendarmes.

As I reached the doorway, Holmes was sprinting across the road, causing the driver of an approaching cab to pull up sharply. As I followed, I was briefly aware of a uniformed man off to my right being berated in no uncertain terms for his appalling blunder in loosing off a shot. Over his shoulder, Holmes shouted: "Von Bork appeared momentarily at the door just as I was examining the portal through the glasses. Despite strict instructions, some idiot of a gendarme fired at him. The whole game may have been given away!" Reaching the other pavement, he hurled himself against the closed door, and in a moment I was at his side to add my weight to the pressure he was already applying. The thick timbers resisted our combined efforts at first, but such was our strength in this vital moment that I believe a stone wall would have fallen before our assault. With a groan, the door gave way and Holmes and I pounded forward into the hallway and up a flight of stairs. As we did so, I was conscious of hearing a door slam shut somewhere below us, but the main focus of my attention was the door now facing us on the landing. From within I heard hurried movements.

"Watson, the lock!" cried Sherlock Holmes standing aside from the door. I levelled my revolver and fired twice, shattering the metal lock. Holmes grasped the handle and pushed the door open.

My recollections of the ensuing seconds are necessarily vague and confused, as I was partially blocked by Holmes's form in the doorway. I saw a man jump back from a table piled high, it seemed, with packing cases, and put a pistol to his head. I heard a word shouted in a guttural voice, then saw the flash of a shot. The man's head was wrenched across by the force of the bloody impact; he staggered and fell. Holmes stepped across to the prone body, then moved over to the table at which the man had been seated only a few seconds earlier.

"Holmes, be careful!" I called sharply, for I had seen the glint of a light in the equipment on the table. "It could be a bomb!" But Holmes did not seem to heed my warning and proceeded to tap his index finger on the table.

La Fallière and several police officers had arrived on the scene and clustered in the doorway, staring at the bleeding corpse and the resolute figure of Sherlock Holmes. My friend turned to face them. "Von Bork has escaped. Spread out and find him!" The last two words were spat out in a fury I had seldom seen Holmes possess. Unsure for an instant, the gendarmes looked to their superior for confirmation, then, as he nodded, they disappeared down the stairs, La Fallière following them. Holmes crossed to the window and stared outside.

"There they go, like so many rabbits!" he said bitterly. "We had them in the palm of our hand had not some blind fool pulled his trigger. Now we have lost Von Bork once more, and still do not know if the information he held has been passed on. It is, of course, clear to you what has taken place, Watson?" he queried, turning to me. I had to confess that I was still in the dark.

"The dead man there is Lubin - the contact in Paris, and clearly a man under orders not to permit himself to be captured. Hence his suicide as we entered. I thank you for your fears for my safety, Watson, but this on the table is no bomb; rather, it is a highly complex radio set, similar to those in the Diogenes war-room.

"Clearly, Von Bork arrived here in this building a short time ago and presumably communicated his information to Lubin, who may or may not have had time to send the details by Morse to his superiors before our unexpected appearance. I fear the worst, as the accumulators were connected when we arrived, and the equipment was obviously ready for use. Now, with Lubin dead and Von Bork escaped again, we cannot know if the Kaiser is at this very moment being informed of events and the identity of our man at his side. As you may have seen, I tapped out a few final words in German on the transmitter, indicating, if Lubin had been in mid-transmission when he died, that more information may be forthcoming shortly. I have not the time to search out if there is a code used by the German agent in communication with the High Command; there surely must be, and so it would be far too dangerous for me to attempt to contact them and give them some useless and false information, as I might otherwise be tempted to do." Bitterly, he crushed his fists together until the joints stood out pale against his skin. "You are aware, of course, what this fiasco means, Watson?"

I nodded slowly. "We must go to the Kaiser ourselves, Holmes. We cannot take the risk that Lubin has not given away the vital information, and the safety of our agent there is of the most paramount importance. And besides, Von Bork has escaped again and may himself now try to cross the lines."

Holmes laughed shortly. "That I doubt, Watson. His face by now is far too well known, and descriptions will be at every point in the Allied lines within two hours from now. La Fallière will see to that. No, I fear my enemy will now devote himself entirely to another sphere of activity. But of course you are right: we must make plans for travelling to the front lines, somehow cross over into territory controlled by the Germans, and reach the Kaiser's side at Lombez. Three days ago in Baker Street, you may recall, I was complaining about the lack of activity," he commented wryly. "Now I think we have action enough to suit two men half our age."

He passed out of the room as a police surgeon entered to examine the body of our adversary. But I could no longer concentrate on the events I had just witnessed; turning over and over in my mind was Holmes's last remark about Von Bork's new sphere of activity, and I understood clearly what that meant. The German was now going to kill Holmes, and perhaps myself. Of that there could be no shadow of a doubt.

The Eiffel Tower

As we emerged from the house in the rue Valette, a small crowd had gathered on the pavements on both sides, attracted doubtless by the sound of gunfire and the intense gendarme activity. Looking neither to right nor left, Holmes strode across the road to speak to La Fallière, who was still giving orders to subordinate officers. But the Prefect spoke first.

"I have men everywhere searching the environs. It is most unlikely that he will escape a second time. But we have achieved a success, Monsieur Holmes, no? Lubin is dead."

Holmes cut in brusquely. "Dead, yes, La Fallière; but we have no way of knowing whether he was able to transmit the information he gained from Von Bork. In the long run, certainly it is advantageous for you that Lubin can operate no more, although when they come to hear of the incident, the Germans will no doubt rectify his absence. They cannot long afford to have no senior agent in Paris. But as for how things stand at present, no, *Monsieur le Préfet*, it is decidedly not a success. My friend the doctor and I must make our way to the front line and cross to the enemy side."

The Frenchman stretched out his hands in an attitude of amazement. *"Mais c'est fou, ça.* Ah, pardon me, *Monsieur*, but this is madness you are speaking."

"That is as may be," remarked Holmes, unperturbed. "Nevertheless, it *must* be."

La Fallière shrugged in incomprehension. "If you say so, *monsieur*. I shall consult with Sir Francis Bertie and our front-line commands and see what can be done. In the meanwhile, will you return with me now, so that a report on tonight's activities may be drawn up to your satisfaction?"

Holmes nodded cursorily. "My presence here now cannot contribute anything, I fancy. I shall leave Von Bork's apprehension in the capable hands of your officers." The sarcasm was not lost on the Prefect of Police and he winced. Brushing away some snow that had accumulated in the brim of his hat during the short conversation, Holmes moved wordlessly towards the Prefect's official car which had drawn up at the scene.

While we sped towards the river, the snow abated a little, and as darkness fell, Paris seemed transformed. Tables and shades had hurriedly been brought in from the pavements outside cafés, the streets had cleared of shoppers, and a tranquil carpeted peace had fallen on the city. As we slowed down at an intersection by the Seine, I saw the great river shimmering frostily in the light of a thousand lamps. A pleasure boat moved lazily upstream bearing a number of roisterers: I could not tell if they were still celebrating an extraordinarily late luncheon, or had embarked early on an evening's entertainment.

As I was thus musing on my surroundings, Holmes and La Fallière had been conversing earnestly, the Prefect writing occasional notes in his pocket book.

"I think that should be the way to describe it," said Holmes, "and, of course, you must tread a knife-edge with members of the press. It is reasonable to make capital out of Lubin's death, but too much crowing in official quarters might lead to German reprisal action."

The Prefect nodded in agreement and snapped his book shut. "In that case, Monsieur Holmes, *Monsieur le Docteur*, I would suggest that my driver takes these instructions to my secretary and he will draft both an official report and a statement to the newspapers. He can also telephone the correct channels to prepare for your expedition to the lines. But meanwhile, may I offer you a *petit boisson*, perhaps at our famous landmark, the Eiffel Tower? If the bar on the second stage has closed, I may reopen it by special police decree!" He chuckled at the awareness of his powers. Holmes smiled drily. "Besides, the view over Paris with the veil of snow around her visage, will be something rather special, I think."

"Well, Watson, are you game for a brandy at four hundred feet?" Holmes asked with a twinkle in his eyes.

"Despite your disgraceful insinuations to Miss Polly Dempster about my drinking habits, Holmes, I am perfectly happy to accept the Prefect's invitation. Brandy or not, it will add a touch of poetry to a day replete enough with action."

"Then we both accept, La Fallière," said Holmes. "I presume we shall be contacted if Von Bork is by any chance captured?"

"But yes, indeed!" replied the Prefect, again aware of the intended sarcasm.

Our car drew to a halt as we were about to cross the bridge to the

Île de la Cité, and Holmes and I got out. La Fallière spent a few minutes giving detailed instructions to his driver; then he too came out, and the car moved off into the darkness.

"It is a walk of no more than twenty minutes, and worth it, I believe, gentlemen," said the Prefect, and we both nodded in approbation. However, as we started, my eye was caught by a single bookstall hard up against the embankment wall that had been kept open by its owner despite the bad weather. Always on the lookout for interesting volumes, I told my companions that I would catch them up in a few minutes, and crossed to the display.

I spent a short but interesting time at the stall, discussing the merits of Jules Verne, as opposed to our own H. G. Wells, as visionary authors, and as an example of my equivocation on the subject, came away with cheap French copies of both writers. Bidding farewell to the affable man at the stall, I began to hurry after my friends, whose figures I could dimly see progressing at leisurely pace along the river walk.

I was about to hail them when I saw something rather strange. Holmes and La Fallière were perhaps thirty paces ahead of me, deep in conversation, their shadows thrown long behind them on the snow from a street lamp. And yet it seemed to me that another shadow merged with theirs for an instant, then faded. I tried to pierce the gloom. It came again, and this time I fancied I perceived a movement along the trees bordering the pavement. Taking the precaution to slip into the line of trees myself, I edged forward. Again there came a movement, as a dark shape detached itself from the deeper black surroundings. All oblivious, Holmes and La Fallière continued on their way, still deep in their discussion. I approached the spot where I believed I had first seen the shadow. Surely enough, prints were clearly visible, the marks of thin, pointed boots flitting from cover to cover in pursuit of the two lone figures ahead. I looked up again, ready now for action at any moment, and what I saw caused me straightaway to loose my revolver in my pocket and release the catch. A shaft of light from a street lamp where, perhaps, the gas-jet was higher than usual, arched across the pavement, and caught the mysterious tracker in a momentary pool of light. I saw him for no more than half a second, but that glimpse was enough to show me the aquiline features, the heavy, cruel eyebrows, the hunched shoulders, of a man I had last seen on an August night that year, when I had helped Sherlock Holmes smash the German spy ring in England.

Von Bork was on the trail just as Holmes had envisaged.

My grip tightened on the handle of my Webley as I sized up this new and dangerous situation. Clearly, I should not show myself and call Holmes's attention to his pursuer, lest Von Bork be panicked into precipitate action. Presumably, also, the German would not choose to act in so public a place: he was following until a suitable time and spot showed themselves. The tracker himself tracked - it appealed to my literary sense, and inwardly I smiled.

Thus we progressed along the edge of the Seine - Holmes and his companion walking and chatting amiably, a shadow in the trees some twenty yards behind them, and another, perhaps thicker-set shadow following as best and as quietly as he might, a further few yards in the rear. Fortunately the pavement was entirely deserted: the inclement weather had driven Parisians into the warmth of their homes, otherwise our strange procession must have been noticed and commented upon. In a few minutes, we swept to the left, as the pavement followed the course of the river. Lights winked in the windows of the great government buildings on the other side of the broad road, but my attention was firmly fixed on what was going on before me.

And then we had reached our objective. Perhaps two hundred yards away down a wide gravelled causeway, a thousand tiny lights picked out the shape of the four enormous uprights of the tower built by Eiffel only twenty-five years previously. I had seen it once, but never in the dark, and it was a truly magnificent sight, rearing high above us, the intricate tracery of the ironwork clearly seen with the help of the lights that covered the monument from its base to the wireless mast at its topmost point, nearly a thousand feet in the sky.

A few casual passersby were to be seen strolling beneath the Tower, perhaps leaving it after ascending to one of the viewing platforms. Attendants and gendarmes were busily engaged in closing off the entrances and exits to the steps and lifts, but I saw La Fallière engage one of them in brief conversation, then proceed with Holmes into a lift. Von Bork had been sheltering in the cover of a souvenir stall, its wares carefully locked away behind shutters, but he slipped forward as the lift containing my friends began its slow progress upwards and, pressing himself behind an iron stanchion, chose his moment when the guard was not watching carefully, and sidled through the entrance and up the first few steps. I moved forward from my cover, but a sixth sense told me to pull back into the shadows again, and it was as well that I did so. The German, safely past the first line of defence in the form of the gendarme, turned suddenly on the steps and glanced backwards. I pressed myself against the trunk of a tree, a mere fifteen paces from the gateway. Then he turned as if satisfied and started to climb.

I, in my turn, watched the gendarme and chose my moment. Perhaps I took a risk in moving so quickly, but it was essential that I keep Von Bork in view, to prevent the dastardly plot he had laid that might end in the destruction of my friend. The guard noticed nothing and I made a mental note to mention his rather lackadaisical attitude to the Prefect. Onward and upward I followed the German, trying always to match my footfall on the metal steps with his above me, so that he might not hear me. In this I was successful, and Von Bork continued on his chase, completely unaware of my presence. It was a fatiguing ascent and I heartily envied Holmes and La Fallière in their smooth conveyance. I heard their voices of a sudden above me, as they stepped out of the lift. Holmes was evidently talking about my absence.

"... he knows our destination, my dear La Fallière, and you instructed the gendarme at the entrance to let him pass. But what a stupendous view we have here." Their voices faded away, as the Prefect replied that they would go on up to the bar on the second stage. I heard the soft foot steps of Von Bork ascend the remaining stairs, and I hurried upwards.

In five more exhausting minutes, we reached the second viewing platform, high above Paris. As I paused for an instant to rest and collect my thoughts, ready for the struggle that must inevitably come very soon, I heard the ringing of glasses and the enthusiastic comments of the barman, who was surprised and proud to have so eminent a guest as the Prefect of Police. The platform was little more than thirty yards square, with a refreshments stall in addition to the bar. A great illuminated clock, its hands pointing to a few minutes before seven, dominated the drinking area. For a moment I lost Von Bork in the darkness, but the lights set around the clock picked him out as surely as if they were aimed at him. I followed him round the platform as the German tried to settle on a position from which to strike at the two conversing men. Inching along, his hand upon the guardrail that was set at an absurdly low level, the spy felt his way around a corner and into a narrow space between the rail and a side of the bar structure. I was only a few feet from him now, and I crouched low behind a packing case full of empty bottles.

Sherlock Holmes and the Prefect were seated at a table close to the bar, not talking now, but settled comfortably and sipping their brandies. The waiter busied himself with drying some glasses and putting his stall to rights after what had doubtless been an energetic day for him. Whatever the weather was now, I recalled that earlier it had been a most pleasant winter's day.

"I must say, La Fallière," Holmes began easily leaning forward and putting his glass on the table "Lubin has been a remarkably successful agent hitherto..." His comment went unfinished, for at that very instant, Von Bork made his move. He lunged forward, a flash of steel in his hand. I had been mentally preparing myself for such an action for the last half-hour or so, and I was equal to the emergency.

"Holmes, look out!" I cried as I launched myself at Von Bork's back.

The scene will forever remain etched in my memory. La Fallière sat rigidly in his chair, his glass inches from an astonished mouth; Sherlock Holmes, with panther-like reflexes, was already rising, arm outstretched to protect himself from the impending blow; the demented form of Von Bork leaping forward, the long blade in his hand snaking towards my friend's chest. I grasped the German's collar desperately and, at the last possible moment before he would have struck Holmes, brought my pistol crashing down upon his skull. Von Bork's knees seemed to buckle under the force of the blow and he staggered forward, still clutching the knife, but now seemingly unaware of his target. Blood poured from the wound in his head, matting the grey hair and spilling downwards onto his overcoat. Holmes stretched out a hand, but sharply withdrew it as his assailant slashed viciously with his blade. Then the German, driven into a blind frenzy by the pain and total unexpectedness of my assault, turned suddenly and lurched towards me.

"Watson, for God's sake move aside!" called Holmes. I did as he bade and stepped to one side as Von Bork leaped forward. The impetus of his lunge carried him on past me, but he managed to whip the knife in my direction as he staggered on, and an agonizing pain seared through my shoulder. I slumped backwards and could only be a passive witness to the events of the next few seconds. Holmes moved towards me; La Fallière, by this time shaken into action, was blowing a whistle with all his might as he advanced on Von Bork, drawing his revolver from its holster. An appalling shriek from the German wrenched my head in his direction. The force of his charge at me had carried him to the very limit of the platform. The handrail struck him a sickening blow in the pit of his stomach; he sagged back under the impact, then slowly, so slowly it seemed, crumpled forwards. I think he must for a shattering moment have understood his fate, for he shook his head blindly and his hands traced dumb patterns in the night air. But, as La Fallière reached him, he fell forward over the rail arms flailing pathetically. A last scream, and he surged downwards out of my sight. La Fallière made a final swing over the edge that almost caused his downfall also, but he gripped the rail fiercely and hauled himself back. Utter silence, shocked horror upon our faces: Holmes gaunt and pale, bending low over me: La Fallière motionless against the inky blackness of the night, looking down: the waiter struggling to his feet. Then we all heard a dull thud far below us and surprised shouts and cries.

"Watson, for God's sake, tell me that you are all right!" said Holmes urgently.

I felt my shoulder. "No matter, Holmes; it was only a glancing blow. It was more the shock of the impact that knocked me down. But Von Bork ... "

Holmes nodded, a queer look on his face. "Thank you, my dear friend, thank you." He looked away and raised a hand to his eyes. I swallowed with emotion.

"It's been a long day, Watson, " said Holmes, aiding me to my feet.

Troop Train to the Front

I awoke the next morning, extraordinarily refreshed by the luxury of twelve hours' sleep. My wound of the previous evening had been bandaged and, despite my protestations, Holmes had insisted that I return with no further ado to the Hotel Wagram; there, Monsieur Dalmy had been as solicitous as might have been expected, fussily attentive to my every need. I gathered from Holmes that he and La Fallière had returned to the Prefecture to draw up a second report, that on Von Bork's death. Lubin's demise, it had already been decided, could not be kept out of the newspapers because of the attendant police activity in a public street in daylight; but the circumstances of Von Bork's death had been somewhat different, and it was not felt necessary to release anything to waiting reporters other than a brief note to the effect that an unknown man had met his end in falling from the second stage of the Eiffel Tower. If they then chose to make anything of the fact that the Prefect of Police had by chance been taking a drink nearby, that was entirely their business.

Over breakfast, Holmes told me he had also seen the Ambassador late the previous night, and had received the proper clearances for us to travel up to the front line in a troop train.

"But are you sure that you are fit enough to travel, Watson?" he asked, attacking his third egg.

"Never felt fitter in my life, my dear Holmes," I replied, then retracted a little as my companion looked up questioningly. "Well, it does ache somewhat, but nothing will keep me from accompanying you on this final phase of our adventure."

"Ah, so it is an adventure now, is it?" laughed Holmes. "No doubt you are already in contact with your agent, Doyle, and have arranged a sizeable advance payment!"

But soon the practical needs of the day returned us to the pressing urgency of our situation. Sir Francis Bertie had confirmed to Holmes that, as far as our intelligence knew, the Kaiser and his staff were installed in a large château at Lombez, a few miles behind the German lines. Thence he would emerge each day, and with the Christmas season already abroad, would travel around various units of his immense forces, exhorting his men to greater efforts. Poring over large-scale detailed maps at the Embassy, Holmes pinpointed Lombez and was thus able to select the nearest relevant section of our own lines to which we should make our way.

"I think the entrenchments by the village of Fleurbaix must be our goal, Watson. Our line at that point is closer to the Germans than at almost any other place along the front. A mere hundred and forty yards separate the combatants. Recently, too, it has been a relatively peaceful section of the line, a fact which should make our crossing of No Man's Land that much easier; and then it is a walk of a few hours to Lombez. As to how we shall approach the task of crossing, I cannot tell until we are actually in the British line. Although I now owe it to you to save your life in return for last night's incident, it would be unwise to court more than the necessary minimum of danger. At three o'clock this afternoon, a troop train leaves from the Gare du Nord for Arras by way of Amiens. From Arras, it will not be too long a journey by motor to the line at Fleurbaix. Until this afternoon, then, we must find our own amusements."

Our remaining hours in the French capital were spent by me in an attitude of frustration and anticipation. While Holmes disappeared once more, this time to transmit a message to Mycroft in the Diogenes war-room, informing him of our newest plans, I again tried to read my frail adventure novel, but, quickly growing bored, settled down to write some coherent notes on the frantic events of the past four days. I tired even of this when I found myself speculating on the eventual outcome of the case rather than remembering facts that were already in the past.

The time passed slowly, and it seemed an age until, shortly before half past two, a cab was at the door of the hotel, awaiting Holmes and myself. Both of us promised Monsieur Dalmy, under intense pressure, that we would return as soon as things improved after the war; then, as the commissionaire placed our baggage in the rear, we moved off up the rue de Rivoli.

Holmes sorted through a small pile of papers in his lap. "A pass for the train ... documents signed by Bertie and La Fallière establishing our identities ... a note from G.H.Q. Intelligence in Paris ... and what amounts virtually to a free pass for anywhere we wish to go under British jurisdiction, signed by as senior a general officer as could be found in Paris on the receipt of brother Mycroft's orders. There, Watson, a fairly comprehensive list, would you not say?" I nodded in assent, while privately thinking that all the paper in the world would be ineffectual in actually helping us out of the Allied lines and into the German. I believe Holmes must suddenly have been struck with the same thought, for he laughed shortly and thrust the sheaf away in the recesses of his coat.

"Partial means towards an end, Watson," he commented laconically, and sat back in his corner.

The station, when we arrived, was a chaos of officers, soldiers, sweethearts and porters. As lines of men waited on the platforms, Holmes and I were waved through the barriers immediately on producing our passes, and we had little difficulty settling ourselves in the correct train, since few soldiers had yet been allowed on. Tears fell in profusion on all sides, handkerchiefs fluttered in farewell, and Holmes, acerbic as ever when the female sex intruded, could not forbear commenting. I have said before that he was never able to speak of the softer passions save with a gibe or a sneer. Sherlock Holmes himself has told me that he thought the criticism a trifle unfair; yet he rarely had a good word to say for any women other than Miss Irene Adler and our worthy housekeeper, Mrs. Hudson.

"I seriously wonder, my dear Watson, if the presence of female companions at the moment of parting does our fighting men any positive good; I am inclined to doubt it. A tear at home in familiar surroundings, when the parting is not so imminent: that may be understood and, in some measure, condoned. But a handkerchief waving and receding as the train pulls away, the image of a tear-stained loving face as the last picture retained by a private soldier of his sweetheart, could well have a negative effect. For my part, I should not permit women within the precincts of a station whence men are travelling to the trenches."

As he finished speaking, an officer manœuvred himself into our compartment, bearing with him two sizeable cases.

"Captain Lockyer, of the East Kents, gentlemen," he said, introducing himself. "I fear I cannot agree with your last sentiment, sir," this last directed at Holmes. My friend briefly looked the young man up and down.

"In your specific case, I think my remark is particularly apposite, captain," said Holmes, chuckling. The man looked down sharply.

"Why, what do you mean by that, sir?" I must confess that I too was surprised by Holmes's statement.

"I would have thought it unlikely that you would wish your two consorts to see each other bidding you farewell. Or perhaps they are already aware of each other's existence?" He raised a quizzical eyebrow. "Tut, sir, pray do not be ruffled."

"While admitting nothing, sir, I should be interested to know the basis for your comment. It is something such as Sherlock Holmes might say in one of his exploits." At this I nearly exploded, but Holmes flashed a warning look, as if to say, "Let us have our fun."

"I perceive that you have two female companions, just as surely as I know that you have been on at least a week's leave in Paris, that you are a regular soldier as opposed to a volunteer, that your knowledge of the French language is greater than might normally be expected of a British officer - probably you picked it up while you were at Oxford - and, finally, despite having seen recent heavy action, you suffer from some little defect of your right eye."

"Good God, sir!" came the rather strangled response from Captain Lockyer.

"Then am I correct in my deductions?" queried Holmes pleasantly.

"Indeed you are, sir. But how in the world are you able to tell so much about a man you have known for under five minutes?" Holmes leaned back as the train gathered speed and drew out of the station, and placed his fingertips together in time-honoured fashion.

"As to your dual loves, I must counsel you, captain, to attend to the washing of your face more assiduously: when the ladies concerned use different shades of lip salve, you may find yourself in trouble one day. Your superior knowledge of French is indicated by the well-thumbed copy of Baudelaire's poems thrust into your tunic, just as your week-long leave is clear from the stub of a *Folies Bergères* ticket of just seven days ago stuck in the band of your cap. I must confess it was something of a long shot to say that you were at Oxford, but you have confirmed it, and, in some measure, that backs up my statement that you are a regular soldier. That, of course, is clear from the fact that already, within only four months of hostilities, you are a captain; and the leather army boots you are wearing could only have come from a certain shoe-maker's in Turl Street, in the university town; I should estimate their age at approximately four years, and yours at twenty-six or seven, which permit of your being up at the University for three years, then purchasing the boots when you entered the army in 1910."

He paused for a moment.

"1909," said the officer, staring at Holmes in amazement.

"Close enough, I fancy. The last two points are, of course, simplicity itself. Recent action is shown by the scorched graze across your shoulder strap - it could only have been caused by the passage of a bullet; and your weak sight, while clearly not serious, leads you to wear a monocle at times - the reddish creases round your eye are quite distinctive."

"Extraordinary," admitted the captain.

"Commonplace," declared my friend.

"May I enquire your name?"

"My name is Sherlock Holmes; may I introduce my companion, Dr. Watson?"

Life and Death in the Trenches

The details of our journey to Arras need not detain me long. After some initial discomfiture when he discovered the true identities of Holmes and myself, Captain Lockyer proved an affable enough travelling companion; and indeed we needed an intelligent conversationalist, for, including a long sojourn at Amiens, our train took close on eighteen hours to reach its destination of Arras. We heard at some length the captain's personal experiences at the front, together with those of his regiment, the East Kents; we dozed on occasions; Holmes fumed with impatience, but eventually realised that nothing would be gained that way and so chose total silence as an alternative.

At Arras, then, we arrived on a bitterly cold morning at nine o'clock and emerged into the small grey town stretching our weary limbs and immediately on the look-out for transport up to the front. Arras still had two years before it was to enter the history books, but now it was a vital staging-post for the Allied front line, constantly being used by men going forward and by casualties being ferried back.

"This is where we shall get the true feeling of war, Watson," murmured Holmes as we stood in the station square, and of course he was right. The Paris we had left a day previously might have been in another continent for all the similarity it bore to a city in wartime.

"Mr. Holmes, Dr. Watson, you are both welcome to journey with me to my billet," said Captain Lockyer. "My men are only a quarter of a mile from the Fleurbaix section of the line, and my batman will have arranged some form of transport for me." Holmes and I gratefully accepted the offer, and the three of us waited while all around us troops milled and formed into columns, finally disappearing along the winding town roads that led eventually to the front. Brave men they were, singing and marching firmly, grimly determined to do their duty many miles from their homes. A corporal appeared suddenly at Lockyer's side and saluted smartly.

"I was sent to tell you, sir, that there ain't no transport up to the line for you, sir; but could you come up to the billet as soon as you can, sir? The colonel says he needs you very bad right now. We lost Captain Marlowe and Lieutenant Shelley yesterday, sir."

Lockyer's face fell. "Killed?"

The corporal looked down. "Lieutenant Shelley got it straight in the 'ead, sir. Didn't use a periscope to look out the trench. The captain ... he ... er ..." The man shifted his ground and looked uneasy.

"Well, out with it, man!" snapped Lockyer.

"I'd rather not, sir; he ... he was right by me when he got it. A Hun shell landed right at 'is feet. There weren't much to pick up, sir." Lockyer swore softly, while Holmes stood stolidly by, staring into the middle distance.

"Anyway, sir," continued the corporal, swallowing in emotion, "we can 'itch a ride in an ambulance or something."

"Where's Johnstone, my batman?" asked the captain.

"Sent back behind the lines two days ago, sir. Lost an arm in a push we made Friday."

My blood ran cold at the matter-of-fact way in which the man detailed this dreadful list, and yet even he, who had seen furious action over the last months, could still be affected when an officer was killed next to him.

"Hark at that, Watson," said Holmes, the first words he had spoken in several minutes. Echoing dully from the north came the unmistakable sound of artillery fire, presumably the regular morning barrage from both sides. Such a sound I had not heard since Maiwand, during the Afghan War and my own term of service in the Fifth Northumberlands.

"The season of goodwill, eh, my friend?" said Holmes, clapping Lockyer on the shoulder. "Two days before Christmas and neither side will let up for an instant. With a gun in his hands and the opportunity to use it, man is an infinitely different creature."

"Why, Holmes, that is pacifist talk," I cried.

My friend nodded. "Indeed it is, Watson, indeed it is. Brood over the twenty miles to the line on what you want to see there, and then gauge how it tallies with the truth. It will be a sobering experience."

I have been reading the daily newspapers in London, Holmes. I hardly feel I am ignorant on the point," I exclaimed.

"Very well, Watson, I shall say no more. Ah, corporal, is that not an ambulance? We may hail a lift from it, perhaps." The man ran out into the station square and halted the vehicle in question. We discovered the ambulance was indeed returning to the front, having recently brought a number of amputees into Arras. And so we continued this last stage of our journey to Fleurbaix.

As the miles passed, so the sound of shelling grew closer and closer. Every now and again we could see dark clouds of smoke billowing into the air, and then, a few seconds later, would come the delayed sound of the explosion. At one point we drove past the gaunt outline of an old house, an outline because it was a mere shell; the four walls had nothing more to contain than rubble and the white flecks of past snowdrifts. A blackened chimney-stack pointed an accusing finger towards the heavens; the bloated shape of a dead cow greeted anyone who chose to loiter where once there had been a door. What had been in Arras a dull, general roar now became a series of individually recognisable explosions as we drove on towards the line; I fancied on several occasions that I even heard the whistle of the shells as they flew on their deadly ways. Neither Captain Lockyer nor his corporal seemed in the slightest degree perturbed. Indeed, the officer looked calmly at his watch.

"Coming up to eleven; this is an unusual pasting. Doesn't normally go on much past ten. Wonder if anything's up." And then, almost as he spoke, the barrage died, leaving only eddies of smoke scudding away on the wind. The ambulance jerked to a halt.

"Well, we're here. The East Kents are in the line about a quarter of a mile away, but from here the line is straight ahead a few hundred yards," said Lockyer, intimating that we should step out.

"But where is Fleurbaix?" I asked. "That was our destination."

"Oh, didn't you see when we went through it, old chap? That hulk with the dead bullock or whatever it was ... that's what's left of the village of Fleurbaix." There seemed little one could say to that; Holmes contented himself merely with thanking the captain and making him an invitation to visit us in Baker Street after the war. Captain Lockyer, we heard years later quite by chance, was blown to fragments at Passchendaele; a previous gallantry award proved no protection against a German grenade in that most desperate of battles.

The ambulance pulled away and we turned to survey the scene. So bleak it was, with shattered, tumble-down sheds serving as cover for supplies and casualties alike; a smashed British gun lay sprawling drunkenly on its side, barrel twisted into unimaginable shapes, with the bodies of two gunners intertwined in the wreckage; a stretcher case lay outside one of the lean-tos, crying softly as a medical orderly who could not have been more than twenty years of age tried to help him - a ragged private soldier, presumably a friend of the wounded man, stood beside the orderly, leaning against a shattered wall; incongruously in this picture of destruction, several piles of gleaming new barbed wire lay coiled beneath the branchless trunk of a tree - looking more closely, I saw a soldier's cap embedded in a fork of the tree. Underfoot the earth had been churned into a frenzied morass: the recent cold weather had frozen the mud rock-hard, so that horses drawing a passing gun caisson had to pick their way delicately along the track for fear of harming their hooves.

An officer bustled up to us. "What the hell are you doing here? Are you civilians? Go to the rear immediately." Holmes brought out the sheaf of documents he had procured for just such an eventuality.

"A brief look at these papers will, I think, convince you of our purpose, major. What regiment is posted in this section? I should like to see the commanding officer." The major glanced over the permits and letters of transit, then looked up with new respect in his face.

"I'm sorry, gentlemen, to have been so short with you. Will you come with me?" Holmes smiled graciously and we followed the officer over towards a low ridge of earth. Here began one of the many communication trenches that led to the front line, and we carefully picked our way down a makeshift ladder onto the duckboards that had almost obligatorily to be laid at the bottom of trenches to provide any form of safe footing. Nevertheless, in several places as we made our way forward, the boards seemed to give way as I stepped on them, floating for a moment on inches of mud that had not frozen, causing me to lose my balance and grasp at the walls of the trench for support. A slight commotion alerted us to stand back against the side; a stretcher borne by two men was huriedly taken past us, with the wounded fellow in dreadful pain. The major ran his fingers through his hair in distracted fashion.

"The Hun kept up their guns for much longer than usual this morning; you probably heard them still firing as you came up. They lulled us a bit by pretending to end their barrage at about the normal time, so our guns stopped. Then they opened up again ten minutes later and caught several of us on the hop. Come, gentlemen, we're nearly there." Abruptly we turned to our right and found ourselves in a somewhat wider trench, but just as filthy as the first. Sandbags lay piled along the top of the left-hand ridge of the trench, broken at intervals by small embrasures, through which pointed the thin metal tubes that I knew to be periscopes, a means of seeing the activities of the enemy over the level of the trench without showing oneself. Other slits were manned by taciturn soldiers with what seemed to me outsize rifles, with telescopic sight additions to them. Eagle-eyed, these men leaned forward, peering through the sights, the butts of their weapons pressed so comfortably into their shoulders that one could have recognised the hardened veteran before any form of introduction. As we passed one of them, I saw him suddenly make a slight adjustment to his sights, then pause for a moment before loosing off a single shot that echoed eerily around us, the only sound of gunfire in the vicinity. For an instant more he checked through his lens, then stepped back, apparently satisfied with his work.

"Bastard 'ad already shown hisself over the top once - 'e didn't ought to 'ave done that. Oh, pardon me, sir!" He sprang to attention as the major, followed by Holmes and myself, came level with him. "I didn't know as there was an officer near, sir."

The major smiled. "No matter, Dorling; got another one?" The man nodded laconically. "Keep up the good work, then." As we passed out of the soldier's earshot, the major whispered to us:

"Sharpshooters: marvellous chaps they are, and bloody terrifying. Dorling and a few others like him can guarantee to kill if a man shows himself for more than a second and a half."

A brief interview with the rather pompous colonel of the regiment was enough to satisfy him of our purpose, and once he had been enjoined not to tell any others of our mission, Holmes indicated our somewhat dirty condition and asked where we might be billetted. The colonel immediately gave instructions to the guard at the entrance to his dug-out - really no more than a deep hole cut into the side of the trench - and within a few minutes we were being conducted further along the line towards what we were assured was the most comfortable billet in this section of the trenches. I had feared that this would prove to be a relative comparison, and so indeed it turned out: a dug-out that could literally not hold anything more than two bunks and a table. A chipped placard stuck into the mud outside announced that we were to move into 'Sleepy Hollow', a pointer to the sense of humour of the two junior officers whom we were causing to move out of their quarters. Holmes tried to apologise, saying that he hoped it would only be for one night, but the two lieutenants did not seem annoyed.

"This has been our sixth billet in as many weeks, sir," said one of them. "I think we're used to it by now. Anyway, I gather that you're some kind of undercover people on a special mission, so I suppose it's important."

Holmes chuckled. "Oh yes, lieutenant, I think you might say that." He paused, then seemed to remember something. "Tell me, when does it get dark now?"

"Round about five, sir. I was out last night with a wire party and we left the line just about then; didn't stop the Hun, though. He must have got wind of something and sent up a star shell about half an hour later; took us completely by surprise and they were able to set a machine-gun on us before we knew what was happening. They got two of my men. It was a bloody mess of an operation in all, sir, and the colonel's now said that we must keep out of No Man's Land tonight. Actually that doesn't matter. All the wiring is nearly done."

Holmes put down his bag with an expression of annoyance. "Yet another delay, Watson," he said, turning to me. "We cannot risk the safety of the men in this section by attempting to cross tonight: if the Germans are already on the *qui vive* after last night, then it would be irresponsible both for our own skins and for future operations by the men here. Another chance to cool our heels, then."

Holmes may have chosen to use that expression, but our experience over the next day and a half showed us that daily life in the front line was anything but cool. On four separate occasions the men in our section were stood to arms when a German attack seemed suddenly to threaten. But none materialised and the men, grumbling and grousing, would return to whatever they had been doing before the alert came. Some played cards endlessly, gambling initially for cigarettes - that most important item of currency - then proceeding to give each other astronomical notes of credit, to be paid, their recipients were assured, just as soon as the war was over. Some others seemed perpetually to doze: men crouched in every possible position, trying to make themselves comfortable, hauling their greatcoats over them to keep out the ceaseless wind and dragging their cloth caps down over their ears. Constant repairs were being made in the trenches, with shell-flattened sleeping quarters being hollowed out anew, and dislodged sandbags being put to rights. Private Dorling and others of his silent breed continued their deadly work at all hours. On the morning of Christmas Eve it started raining and did not let up until the early evening. Sherlock Holmes spent the day sitting disconsolately in our dug-out; I, on the other hand, was keen to capture all the sensations of daily life for our men in the trenches and, despite my age, it seemed that the men were happy enough for me to wander about, observing them at work or at play. As an instance of this I was able to note the happy faces of those who received letters by the post that morning-probably the last delivery for some few days now that the holiday period had begun. The corporal delegated to deliver post sloshed through the driving grey rain, shielding his precious cargo as best he might under a battered cape. At his call of "Letters from home!" men appeared from every corner, like rabbits from a warren. Eager anticipation on all faces, soon to change to ecstatic joy or disillusioned sorrow, expressed far more clearly than their words could ever do the importance of this slender contact with the world they knew outside the horror of northern France.

One peculiarly sobering experience involving me closely occurred shortly after midday on that Christmas Eve. After lunching early Holmes had left to see the colonel to enquire about the prospects for crossing the line that night; thus I was left to my own devices. Pulling over my head a cape that had been acquired for me, I stepped from the cover of our dug-out and moved hurriedly along the trench, anxious to get out of the slashing rain. My goal was a certain lieutenant who had discovered the identities of Holmes and myself and wished to discuss the details of some of our past cases. As it happened, I met the officer in question out on the duckboards and we moved on down the trench towards his dug-out. A machine-gun opened up in the distance, its stuttering fire punctuating the hiss of the constant rain. A group of men a few yards before us were taking shelter from the weather and as we approached them, one of them called out: "Watch out, sir!" I heard the caution, but my companion continued on a few paces; what sense told me that I should not follow I do not know; but suddenly the chatter of the German gun seemed infinitely louder and I saw bullets striking the upper edges of sandbags laid on the lip of the trench.

"Careful, lieutenant!" I shouted, and at that very instant he was hurled back against the side of the trench, pinioned for a moment by the lead that ripped into him. Then the machine-gun traversed on and the lieutenant crumpled slowly down into the mud, clutching at his chest.

The sheltering men leaped forward and piled bags into what I now saw to be a gaping hole in the fortifications - presumably a shell had done the damage in the morning. The lieutenant was bleeding heavily from several wounds in his chest; the breath came heaving from his lungs, and when I saw the tell-tale flecks of red upon his lips, I knew there was nothing to be done to save him. The colour drained from his face, and as I leaned forward to ease his position so that there should not be so much pressure on his chest, he gave a last shuddering sigh and a rush of blood came from his mouth. Rain dashed down upon his sightless eyes and one of the privates drew a cape over the rigid face. The lieutenant had been no more than a boy, perhaps nineteen, possibly twenty.

It had been a sombre experience and I was in no mood to continue my exploration of the trenches. When I returned to our dug-out I found Sherlock Holmes shaking out his waterproof. Briefly, I told him of the young man's death, but no flicker of surprise or sorrow crossed his face.

"Thousands more will die like him, Watson; they it is who must pay the penalty imposed by the squabbles of nations. And yet, perhaps we, by our own efforts tonight, will be able to save a few lives for the future, that they might return to England and start again."

"So we are crossing the line tonight, then?"

"Yes, my dear Watson; we shall spend Christmas Day of this year 1914 behind the enemy lines. Come, see how this German uniform fits you."

No Man's Land

As the hour neared for our attempt, Holmes detailed the plan he had arranged with the colonel. We were both to be dressed in uniforms taken from dead Germans; Holmes carried the identity papers of one Colonel Schumacher, and the uniform found for me had been taken off the body of a Private Schwarz. We were to be accompanied out of the British trenches by a small party of soldiers who would stay with us until we had crossed to halfway through No Man's Land, cutting wire if it impeded us and prepared to give covering fire if we came under attack. Holmes coolly described the next part of the desperate plan.

"When we have reached approximately the half-way point, Watson, the men with us will deliberately loose off a few shots into the air, then turn and get back to the cover of the British line. We in the guise of German soldiers, who have been shot at whilst out on a mission between the lines, must then leg it as quickly as may be towards the opposing lines. Leave any speaking to me, by the by, Watson; I know that you have a grasp of the German language, but I fancy I have the advantage over you." I intimated that I was perfectly happy with the arrangement, while remaining appalled at the deadly danger we would be in.

"I share your concern, but neither I nor the colonel were able to improve on this tenuous scheme. Once in the German trenches it will be to our advantage to remain as calm as possible and ask directions to the rear. I think I shall be able to convince any enquirer that we have been on a vitally important intelligence mission. Then, in the darkness, we begin our journey to the High Command and the Kaiser's entourage at Lombez, thence to spirit away our man at his side."

I let out a rather forced laugh. "My dear Holmes, you speak as if we were about to take a jaunt in Hyde Park."

"A somewhat unfortunate example, Watson; as you are well aware, some of my most dangerous walks in London have been in that park!" A fusillade of shots outside ended our conversation abruptly and I thrust aside the tarpaulin that acted as a door for the dug-out. A sergeant, waving a Lee-Enfield excitedly, shouted:

"No need to worry, sir; just a bit of fun. The Boche has sent one of 'is spotter planes just a bit too close." Holmes joined me at the aperture and we glanced upwards. Directly above us, perhaps a hundred feet up, a biplane was wheeling in the sky, trying to avoid the small-arms fire being directed at it. As I shaded my eyes against the rain that was still falling, I clearly saw the markings on the lower wings, a broad black cross outlined in white. There were two men in it, a pilot and a spotter; but I fancy neither of them had any other thought at that instant than to escape the hot attentions of the British Tommies. Holmes looked on with the air of an interested observer.

"It would be instructive to drive one of those things," was his only comment.

At about a quarter to six the colonel of the regiment came to bid us farewell; the accompanying group of four soldiers were already lounging outside our dug-out, grumbling a little about the extra duty, but sturdy men all, ready to do without question what was asked of them.

"Good luck, gentlemen," said the senior officer, shaking us both by the hand; "You will need it, I fear. I know little of what you propose to do behind the German lines and I am not seeking to know, but it is His Majesty's business, and that is enough."

"What regiment faces us on the German side, colonel?" Holmes cut in sharply.

"The Seventeenth Bavarian Regiment, good fighters all of them," replied the colonel, adding as if a sudden thought had struck him: "Your wound is not troubling you, I hope, doctor? The passage across the lines will be difficult enough as it is without the extra hazard of your knife-wound opening once more." I thanked him for his concern and told him that the injury was already nearly cured by my own ministrations and those of his regiment's medical officer.

"Then we are ready," said Holmes brusquely. The glint of action was in his eyes and he was impatient to start. We stepped outside. The rain, though still falling, had abated its force of earlier in the day, and darkness covered the whole scene. The colonel clapped us both on the shoulder and I checked that I was carrying all I needed tucked beneath the uniform I was wearing. The sergeant in command of our party climbed three wooden steps and raised his head warily over the lip of the trench. For a moment he looked, then, almost soundlessly, pulled himself up and over the top. We waited in breathless silence. No sound came from the German lines. Quickly a second man climbed over, we followed, and the remaining two brought up the rear.

It was a dark world in which we found ourselves. Cut off from the twinkling lights of our own trenches, we could see only by the last faint traces of light fingering across the sky where the sun had gone down some hour earlier. The enemy trenches were only a little over a hundred yards away; indeed, we could hear, carried on the gentle breeze, the sound of pots clattering and voices murmuring. We worked our way slowly forward, pressing our bodies hard into the filth and mud. A mile down the line, a lone machine-gun coughed into action, but it could not possibly affect our progress and so we crawled on. At one point Holmes, who was just in front of me, let out a muted expression of disgust, and I understood why when I in turn let fall my hand on the rotting shreds of flesh left on an almost bare human skull. My gorge rose, but I fought down the sensation of nausea and pressed on. The tension was enormous, so that one almost wished to laugh out loud to break the appalling tightness in the stomach. Holmes touched me on the shoulder.

"Nearly there," came the low whisper. "Ready to start running, old man!" And then we saw a sight that made my blood freeze. Up through the drizzle arched a pink trail of smoke. A pinhead of light began to drop down towards us, and I realised instantly what was about to happen.

"Flatten yourself!" said one of the soldiers behind us urgently. Above us, the pinpoint burst into a great illuminating star of pink light, and a terrific racket broke out a matter of forty yards in front of us as two machine-guns opened up. They traversed all across our section of No Man's Land, spraying us with mud and water, the bullets singing a few feet above our heads.

"Christ, it's no good! They can see us!" burst out one of the Tommies and, scrambling to his feet, he turned and ran. He was cut down within yards, brought crashing on his face into a crater by a veritable explosion of fire. But the unfortunate man had been right. If we lay still where we were we would be picked off, as we were clearly in sight. With the same thought in mind, then, Holmes and I and the remaining three soldiers picked ourselves up.

"Go on, sir," shouted the sergeant, "we'll cover you." Another Very light arced into the sky above us and the sound of the angry guns redoubled in volume. Holmes and I turned and started running for all we were worth. The sergeant and his gallant men then started firing from a crouching position, loosing off as many shots as they could from their rifles in the time. As I charged for the British line I glanced hurriedly over my shoulder, in time to see the sergeant stagger and fall to the ground. His men closed up and started running too. "Hurry, Watson!" called Holmes, a few strides in front of me, and with bullets winging in the air all around us, we stumbled to the parapet of our objective and literally threw ourselves over the edge. For a moment I was stunned and lay there with heaving chest; but Holmes, lithe and active as ever, was on his feet immediately. Anxious men clustered around us and the colonel, whom we had seen only a matter of minutes before, was among them; he commiserated briefly with my companion. Gradually the sound of firing died away, and then I realised that neither of the two soldiers who had survived the initial burst had rejoined us. They too had been shot down. Sherlock Holmes helped me to my feet, his face grim in the light of an oil lamp. His gaunt features, contorted with anger and humiliation, spoke their own story, and I could think of nothing to say, beyond accepting gratefully a warm cup of tea that was thrust into my hands. Holmes waved away a similar gesture and moved off in the direction of the dug-out we had left with such high hopes some fifteen minutes earlier.

I must admit that the shock and strain of.the disastrous escapade caused me to be totally exhausted, and I was more than glad to slump down on the makeshift bed, still wearing the filthy uniform that was to have been my protection behind the enemy lines. And with Holmes seated smoking, the outline of his face picked out by a solitary candle, I sank into a deep sleep.

It did not seem many minutes before I was roughly awakened. I rubbed my eyes and was about to complain most forcibly to Holmes when he placed a finger to his lips and muttered: "Listen!" I sat up on the bed and pulled aside the tarpaulin. For a moment, I could hear nothing, and turned to Holmes for explanation. But he held out a single finger as if transfixed, and then I heard an amazing sound, one that had not been heard before on the Western Front. Borne in on the wind was the sound of singing, and the voices were German. Clearly the words *'Stille Nacht, Heilige Nacht'* floated across the trenches.

"Holmes," I caught my breath, "they're singing 'Silent Night'."

He nodded and brought out his watch; the hands showed just after midnight. "It's Christmas Day, Watson," he whispered. I shook my head in bewilderment, then climbed out of the dug-out. Other British soldiers were slowly emerging from their places of rest, rubbing the slumber out of their eyes and talking in low, whispering voices.

"Look, they've even got a tree," breathed one of them, and indeed, as I peered carefully through an embrasure, I could see tiny lights winking in an unmistakable conical shape. And others sprang up all along the German line, sparkling and delicate. All the while the strains of that most beautiful of hymns came to us on the breeze, and I saw many a man brush away a tear of emotion as we stood, wondering, our thoughts many miles distant. As the German voices died away, a cheery little private cried out: "Here, let's sing 'em something back ... come on!" and a raucous version of a currently popular tune, 'Fred Karno's Army,' was sent over to the enemy in return. A distant German voice could be heard, "Ho la, English; a merry Christmas!"

I turned to Holmes. "They were firing at us a matter of hours ago, Holmes."

My friend hesitated before replying. "They are professional soldiers, but they are ordinary men also."

An officer nearby shouted out to the Germans that we did not wish to shoot on this holy day, and that there should be a Christmas truce. It was an extraordinary suggestion to make, taken, as far as I could see, with no official approbation, but the men around him cheered. He called out again, saying that he would go out into No Man's Land if one of his opposite numbers would do the same.

There was a long silence, then a voice carried distantly, "No shooting?" The officer affirmed this by climbing steadily onto the parapet over which so recently I had precipitously tumbled, and striding into the waste of land between the trenches. We clustered to the edge and craned our heads over. Sure enough, a figure could dimly be seen emerging from the German line and the two men came together and shook hands, a little cautiously, it seemed to me. It was an astonishing spectacle to see two men, made most bitter enemies by their rulers, clasping hands and exchanging the season's greetings in a scene of utter and complete desolation created by the guns they themselves had fired.

The British officer soon returned to our line, with the news that when dawn broke in a few hours he had agreed with his German counterpart that a game of celebratory football should be played by members of the opposing armies. As a Christmas gesture, this was wildly acclaimed by the soldiers, and off they went to their billets, in such spirits that one might have thought peace had been declared.

"What a marvellous thing, Holmes," I said. But I spoke to empty air; Holmes was no longer by my side. I turned around and saw him sitting once more in the dug-out, lost in thought.

Very few of us slept the remainder of that night in this short section of the British line. All were far too excited by the prospect of a day's respite from the routine of war and, more than that, the anticipation of getting to know at close quarters the men they usually saw only at the end of a gun or point of a bayonet. My own mind was so alive with the events of the previous evening, both our attempted crossing of the lines and the marvellous sight at midnight, that I could not possibly get any rest; and I was already enjoying a festive cup of tea, with a measure of brandy poured in, as the first streaks of light stretched across the sky, announcing the advent of dawn. Almost immediately, there was a cry from outside: "They're getting ready; the Huns are coming!"

Holmes pushed me aside as I went to open the tarpaulin. "Wait, Watson, this is the opportunity we've been waiting for. If this game of football, and the general attendant fraternisation, is really going to take place, then we must use it as a cover."

"Good Lord, Holmes; do you mean that we cross into the German lines under the terms of a truce?"

Holmes shrugged. "We shall be doing nobody any harm; we shall not be breaking any pledge. It is too extraordinary an opportunity to be dismissed. Come, put on a British army coat, while keeping on your German uniform, and we shall see the British and Germans at play together."

Still astounded by the enormity of the scheme, I followed Holmes out of the dug-out. Men were already pouring over the parapet of the trenches and walking out into No Man's Land, picking their way through wire and shell-holes. There in the middle they solemnly shook hands and wished each other the compliments of the season. Everyone behaved at first with some degree of reserve, as well they might - wary looks were given when any man made a sudden movement. I joined the queue of men waiting to climb over, then stumbled forward towards this unbelievable scene, pulling the army greatcoat close about me. Sherlock Holmes was on my tail, and the two of us wandered to the centre of the action, laughing and chatting as if we were part of the merry throng.

Across to our right, the wailing notes of a bagpipe started up, soon to be joined by others, and in a moment all the festivities were being conducted to the sound of Scottish music as the band of a Highland regiment celebrated in their own special way. That was perhaps the incongruity that struck me most about this bizarre affair. Soldiers from both armies were laughing and joking with each other, offering small gifts; to my left, a sergeant commented on a counterpart's cigar-case: "Blimey, it's a millionaires' battalion. They've all got loads of bloody cigars!" He accepted a long cheroot from the German amid much merriment and jolly horseplay. Holmes touched my arm and pointed to another group of Tommies and Germans. I could hardly believe my eyes, for their idea of spending a festive time seemed to consist in shaving each other. The soldiers would kneel down and hold up their heads to be shaved - an Englishman to a German, a German to an Englishman. Competing against the strains of the bagpipes came the joint singing of Christmas carols, and it was to the sound of 'Noël' that the long-awaited international football match began.

"Now here our participation in all this ends," whispered Holmes. "This will require extreme care, yet utter bravado. Both of us must shed our outer coats in the piles being made at this moment for the four goal-posts, and then merge into the German section of the crowds, thence back into the German lines. Do it with conviction, Watson, and we are all right. If we are noticed, then not only is it all up with us, but hundreds of young men will experience their most disillusioning Christmas ever." So saying, we walked casually over to a chaotic pile of garments that had been flung off by their owners in the interests of football, and Holmes seemed to stumble for a moment, pitching to the ground. I was about to help him when I saw him rise, in the full uniform of a German colonel; then he was lost among the motley surroundings. My heart in my mouth, I tried to walk calmly along the rough boundaries of play, cheering as the British soldiers created a break. Glancing around for an instant, I saw nobody within ten feet of me and, in one swift movement, let my coat slip to the ground. Then, with never a backward look, I paced meditatively on, following the dim figure of Holmes, whom I saw before me nearing the parapet of the German trenches.

"Ach, Sie sind da, Schwarz!" he greeted me loudly as I drew nearer and, linking arms, we passed over the lip of the trench and climbed down.

There were few German soldiers in the trench; most of them had clambered over and were enjoying the fun in the middle, but those who were there seemed supremely uninterested in us, beyond giving Holmes, in his guise as an officer, a salute. With a flicker of his eyes, my companion indicated a communication trench that joined the front line some yards away. We moved towards it, I followed Holmes at a respectful distance, as befitted my apparent lower rank. Our steps sounded to me immeasurably louder on the duckboards than they were in reality, we rounded the corner, and came face to face with a German corporal who was coming in the opposite direction. He snapped a salute, then was about to pass when he paused and started to engage Holmes in conversation. My German, as Holmes had said, was not particularly strong, and I was completely unable to understand the man as he spoke. With growing horror, I realised that Holmes too was out of his depth. His eyes took on a momentary blank look, such as I have seen when a problem baffles him. He quickly took hold of himself and nodded down at the corporal. My grip tightened on the revolver I had hidden beneath my tunic, and for a moment I contemplated striking at the man, or even shooting him if he was going to interfere with our passage. At close quarters as we were, the sound of a shot would have been entirely muffled, and there were few men nearby to take any notice. Holmes now switched to a peremptory tone of voice and flicked the man's uniform. I understood then the clever way in which he was concealing his ignorance of the corporal's drift: taking advantage of his rank, he was criticising the man's turnout.

"Ihr Name?" he rapped out.

"Kaporal Schickelgruber," replied the man, pulling uneasily at his little moustache. Another few words from Holmes and the little German scuttled off, as if frightened away.

"A close shave, Holmes," I muttered in a low voice. "I was about to shoot the fellow if he continued to be difficult."

"So I saw, my dear Watson. But shooting one minor German corporal must be very low on our list of priorities this Christmas Day. The village of Lombez is not too many miles away: there rest the Kaiser and his followers; there too is our agent, perhaps in deadly danger. Come, the game is just beginning! "

Footprints in the Snow

We walked for the next few hours through scenes of carnage similar to those on the British side of the lines. Indeed, it was impossible at a glance to distinguish between the two opposing armies, the men of each being equally drenched in the slimy grey mud to the exclusion of differences in uniform or regimental markings. I saw Holmes catch my glance and nod in silent agreement.

"Senseless, Watson," he muttered. "This is the monstrous Hun of the propaganda sheets, the defiler of young women and the murderer of babes. Are these beardless, muddy youths the conscienceless killers we read about? If their guns faced east instead of west, would you be able to tell them from our own Tommies?"

It was a question requiring no response, and we continued our purposeful stride in the direction of the village of Lombez. It was no easy walk. The lines had moved back and forth across this area so often in the previous few months that sometimes the road would disappear entirely. Other times it would be cut by a crumbling system of trenches. Everywhere was scattered the debris of war - the ruined cottages, rotting equipment and the bodies of mules cut down by shell or exhaustion. Here and there, crude markers indicated the hurried grave of a fallen soldier; elsewhere the bloated remains of a once proud warrior lay abandoned in the heavy mud of the bleak landscape.

As we progressed, the road took a more recognisable form. It was still heavily used by military traffic and on many occasions we passed convoys of vehicles or columns of marching men; but the land was showing fewer of the ravages that were so apparent nearer the front. By late in the afternoon, we had left the front line area completely and were walking in a country lane, bounded by hedgerows and with woodland on either side.

Sherlock Holmes halted. "I think it would be wise to seek our accommodation for the night, Watson," he said. "I fear there is a chill in the air."

I glanced at the frozen puddles in the roadway and the frost-encrusted bushes on either side and nodded. "A trifle, Holmes," I agreed laconically. "Just a hint of coolness."

A smile creased Sherlock Holmes's face for the first time in several hours. "Good old Watson. Nevertheless, we would be wise to find shelter for the night. It will get considerably colder before the dawn." He paused. "It seems we must take our chances in the woods. I had hoped that we might have reached a village with an inn by now. Unfortunately, the condition of the road slowed us considerably and we are unlikely to discover a tavern for some hours. But it is more than possible we shall find a hut or cottage among these trees."

"Do you think so, Holmes?" I said, puzzled.

"Without a doubt, Watson," he replied decisively. "As we have walked for these past few miles, I have noticed increasing evidence that this area was once an important charcoal-burning centre. You may have noticed frequent cart tracks into the woods on both sides of the road. You will probably have seen the smoky deposits left on trees by the charcoal-burners' fires deeper in the woods. Since such men habitually lived in the area they worked in, I feel reasonably sure that we shall find our accommodation for the night before long." And so saying, he plunged into the undergrowth at the side of the road.

It was as Holmes had reasoned, and within a few minutes we had discovered a derelict building in a clearing. It was the work of a few minutes to plug the holes in the walls with handfuls of earth and collect a plentiful supply of firewood from the ground. Soon we were snug before a blazing fire frying slices of pressed meat from our British army ration packs over the flames. This together with a mug of hot, sweet tea, went some way to restoring me after the hours of walking.

Holmes suddenly gave a sharp exclamation. "Watson, I almost forgot!" he cried and began to rummage in the pack he had carried with him. He triumphantly drew out a flask of brandy. "Well," he remarked, pouring two generous measures, "this is our Christmas dinner, you know. Merry Christmas, old friend."

We raised our metal cups to each other and, as the snow began to fall gently over the forest, we toasted the birth of the infant Christ.

The embers of the fire were still glowing when I awoke in our refuge the following morning. I quickly fanned the ashes back to a small blaze and replenished the hearth from what remained of our firewood. It was only when I looked to the rude couch where Holmes had spent the night that I realised something was wrong. My friend had disappeared. A quick glance was enough to ascertain that the bulk of his equipment was still in the hut. I was baffled. By my watch it was still only eight o'clock in the morning; where could Holmes have decided to go? Could he have considered travelling on to Lombez to warn the agent of his danger without me? Surely not. When I pulled open the rough assembly of boards that passed for a door to the hut, the story became even more perplexing.

There had been a fairly heavy snowfall during the night and tracks were clearly visible. But whereas I had previously simply thought that Holmes had left on some errand of his own, now the problem took on a sinister turn. There were three sets of footprints in the snow, one coming to the hut and two sets going away.

Someone had come in the middle of the night and Sherlock Holmes had left with him. Had he left of his own free will, or had he been compelled to go? And whither had he been taken? It was most odd that I had not been awakened by these comings and goings in the night. Of a sudden a chill swept over me. I realised the implications of the situation in which I now found myself; I was deep behind enemy lines, wearing the uniform of a German soldier and with only a smattering of the German language. If caught, I would almost certainly be shot as a spy, which indeed I had become. But now I was alone and the meagre food supply I had brought in my pack was already running low.

I resolved to prepare breakfast over the blazing fire and consider my course of action. The meal had a great deal in common with the dinner I had enjoyed the previous evening: the same hard biscuit, fried beef and strong tea. As I ate, I reflected. There were several options available to me, but the two strongest calls of duty clashed. Mere self-preservation seemed a short-term rather than long-term objective. Even if I had so wished, and it was the last thing on my mind, I could not return to the safety of England by the route I had come. Crossing the lines was in practice almost impossible; even if I managed to negotiate the German trenches without betraying myself through my lack of knowledge of the language - even if I successfully crossed the wire and shell craters of No Man's Land - I would almost certainly be shot as I advanced, in German uniform, on the British lines.

No, flight was impossible. I had but two choices. The first, and instinctively I felt this was the course I must take, was that I should locate Holmes and rescue him. Another matter for consideration was our mission: essential to the war effort and putting England in the gravest peril if it failed, surely I had a duty to attempt to complete it.

However, I argued to myself that my chances of success in this quarter without Holmes were negligible. The logical answer, of course, was to seek out my companion, and with luck continue together on our mission.

My decision made, I equipped myself with greatcoat and balaclava helmet against the rigours of the now freezing weather and sallied forth to follow the footprints left in the snow. Unfortunately, after a hundred yards the tracks faded into the general slush under the heavy trees. I was unable to pick them up and, remembering that the footprints approaching the hut had come from a different direction, I was on the point of returning to the hut to follow that trail back to its point of origin in the hope of finding some clue to Holmes's whereabouts, when I saw the tracks again. This time they were away to the right and I was eagerly on the trail. I was approaching the road and took out my pistol as a precaution, although I thought it unlikely that the abductors of Sherlock Holmes would still be in the immediate vicinity.

Suddenly, ahead of me, I spotted a slight movement in the under-growth. I froze, then took cover behind a tree trunk. Cautiously peering out, I could see that I had not been mistaken. The bush moved again and this time I caught a glimpse of the crouching figure of a man, his back towards me. Grasping my revolver firmly in my hand, I crept soundlessly towards my quarry in the manner I had learned in Afghanistan those many years ago.

I came within arm's length and reached out my left hand to seize the fellow by the shoulder. This strange person crouching in the forest must surely be the link I needed in the chain of circumstances surrounding the disappearance of Holmes.

My gun trained on the small of his back, grasped his shoulder and pulled violently backwards. I found myself holding an empty German army greatcoat which had been draped over a small shrub. At that instant I was clubbed to the ground by a savage blow to the head. Fortunately my cap and balaclava helmet cushioned the blow to the extent that I was not immediately rendered unconscious. As I fell I twisted on my back, bringing my pistol round to protect myself against further assault. But in the instant of falling I saw my attacker, who had been immediately behind me, hurling himself upon me with renewed force, and to my horror I caught sight of the flashing blade of a long knife or bayonet.

My assailant was on me a fraction after my back struck the snowy ground. I tried to train my pistol and at the same time free my left hand from the folds of the coat that had been left to entrap me. The mysterious figure held his blade high and as it began its flashing descent, the point aimed directly at my heart, I knew that I could raise neither pistol nor arm in time to protect myself from the fatal blow.

Then, in that final moment, realisation dawned as I saw the gaunt face above me. "Holmes! Stop!" I screamed.

The blade halted its arcing plunge a half inch from my chest and an ashen-faced Sherlock Holmes gripped me by the arm. "Watson? Why, what are you doing prowling out here? My dear fellow, I might have killed you!" Rarely had I seen Holmes so shaken. He helped me to my feet and it was only then that I remembered my fears of half an hour before. "Thank God I found you, Holmes!" I cried. "Are you all right?"

My friend raised a hand. "Rather I should ask that of you," he said. "That was a tremendous crack on the head I gave you. But when I spotted someone creeping after me through the forest I naturally feared the worst. And then seeing you in German uniform, your features obscured by that strange woollen helmet and the uniform cap, I did not recognise you. Anywhere else and I would instantly have recognised your gait, but stumbling through the forest in a crouching position, it was impossible. I assumed you were the enemy, old fellow, and, I regret to say, took action accordingly. But you must let me take a look at the injury I have so inadvertently caused you."

I waved away his ministrations. "It is nothing now that I know you are safe, Holmes," I said.

Holmes fixed me with a quizzical stare. "You were afraid for my safety?" he asked.

I nodded vigorously, sending an array of brightly-coloured stars coursing round in my head. "Indeed I was, Holmes. Once I saw you had gone and noticed the tracks, the conclusion was obvious. You had been abducted; thus I resolved to find you and free you so that we could continue in our mission."

Sherlock Holmes took my elbow as we commenced to walk in the direction of the charcoal burner's hut. "I think, Watson, we had, better take this little discourse somewhat more slowly. Now I understand that you awoke and found me missing, or rather, that I was no longer in the hut. What happened next to dispatch you on this rescue mission?"

I eagerly began my story. "When I found you absent I opened the door of the hut. There were three sets of footprints in the snow - one set coming to the hut and two sets leaving it. Using your own methods, Holmes, I deduced, since the snow had not been there when we arrived last night, that someone had arrived during the night and you had left with him."

Holmes nodded approvingly. "Excellent, Watson, excellent. And then?"

"I further deduced that you must have gone unwillingly or under threat. Otherwise you would surely have awakened me to tell me of your plan."

"This is really amazing," said my friend with a note of awe in his voice. "What did you do then?"

"I tracked you through the woods by your footprints and, well, the rest you know," I concluded. "But who was your abductor? How did he force you to go with him and how did you manage to free yourself?"

We had now come within sight of the hut and Sherlock Holmes halted. "That can wait for a moment," he said. "Now, I want your help in a small experiment.''

"An experiment, Holmes?" I protested. "But surely there are more pressing matters; was it the Germans who captured you?"

My friend waved aside my objections. "If you would, just walk to the door of the hut, Watson," he persisted.

"Really, Holmes," I began, but seeing that nothing would sway him from his little game, I reluctantly agreed.

"Before you begin," he added, "I want you to remember to keep clear of the tracks that are already there in the snow."

I looked at the hut and the four tracks leading to or starting from the door - the mysterious three that had been there when I first opened the door in the morning, and the lone set of prints I myself had left when I went in search of Holmes. "Oh, very well," I muttered, in no grand humour, and stamped off towards the hut, leaving Sherlock Holmes some fifty yards distant. When I reached the dilapidated structure I turned towards my companion.

"Now, if you just wouldn't mind coming back here," he called cheerily. I trudged back to him.

"Look, Holmes, would you tell me what all this is about?" I demanded.

He smiled. "Of course, Watson. I just wanted to demonstrate something. You remember what you saw when you opened the door this morning?"

"Of course I do three sets of footprints, one leading to the hut and two leading away."

My friend nodded with satisfaction. "Now, look again and tell me what you see." I turned back to the hut and looked at the footprints in the snow. There were the original three tracks that I had seen and now there were three more of my own.

"Do you not see?" cried a delighted Holmes. "Three further sets, and all your own. Yet they show one set going to the hut and two sets going away as well. You made the first track when you left the hut in search of me; the next you made going back just now, and the final set you have made in returning to where you stand now."

"But," I began in some little confusion, "you mean you made all the sets of prints, you were not abducted, and I took this crack on my head for nothing?"

Sherlock Holmes shook with silent mirth. "Just so," he said. "I merely went out before you awoke, returned while you were still sleeping and then went out again. No mysterious nocturnal visitor, no armed kidnapper - nothing more than a simple scouting expedition." At that, Holmes collapsed in a paroxysm of laughter.

"Really, Holmes," I said indignantly, "it is hardly a matter for such extremes of humour. It was a mistake that anyone could easily have made."

Leutnant von Richthofen

"We are about fifteen miles from Lombez," said Sherlock Holmes, between mouthfuls of the now rather tedious pressed beef. "I propose that we should arrive there in the middle of this afternoon. That will enable us to find lodgings and then make a tour of the village. Once we have the lie of the land we should be able to make positive steps to locate the British agent and warn him of the danger. I pray that we shall be in time."

We were still in the hut in the forest. Holmes had insisted on returning here to eat a meal and consult his maps before we left on the final stage of our journey to the headquarters of the Kaiser. As we sat on the earthen floor he explained what he had been doing in the forest earlier.

"I rose at first light and decided upon a reconnaissance of our surroundings. This was fairly quickly achieved, and I returned here to find you still sleeping. Almost as soon as I returned to the hut I heard the sound of motor engines on the road and I went out again to take a look. There was indeed a convoy of vehicles carrying equipment toward the front. I settled down to keep observation and remained until I heard you blundering along in my wake."

"I really don't think we need go into that again," I said somewhat sheepishly. "I think we had better continue with our assigned task."

We quit the hut about half an hour later and were soon trudging the slushy lane in the direction of Lombez. We had been walking for less than a quarter of an hour when we heard the sound of motor car approaching. It was heading in the same direction as ourselves and we stood close to the side of the road to allow the vehicle to pass. However, it halted beside us, and the driver, a young German officer with a shock of fair curly hair, leaped out. Catching sight of the badges of rank worn by Holmes, the young man threw a smart salute and came sharply to attention.

"Good day, Leutnant," snapped Holmes, returning the salute. "Why have you stopped?"

"It was my intention to offer you a lift, Herr Oberst," said the young officer. "It is an unpleasant day to walk."

Holmes nodded. "That is most civil of you," he said. "We are going to the village of Lombez if that is on your way."

The fair-haired young man nodded vigorously. "Why yes, that is my destination also. I am stationed there."

We climbed into the young man's car, Holmes sitting alongside the driver's seat. I sat in the back with the luggage, as befitted my lowly station of officer's servant.

The young officer was obviously making an effort to be friendly, and, surprisingly, showed none of the customary deference of a subaltern in the presence of a full colonel. "My name is Manfred von Richthofen," he said with a cheery grin before restarting the engine.

Holmes introduced himself as Colonel Schumacher, and with a wave of a hand remarked that the person riding in the back was his servant, First Class Private Schwarz. Von Richthofen was clearly curious as to why a colonel and his orderly came to be walking along a country lane well behind the lines in France.

Holmes began telling a story we had rehearsed earlier. "We were at the front making certain observations," he said. "In the confusion of an attack we became separated from our companions and I decided to press on alone."

"Are you stationed near here?" asked von Richthofen.

Holmes smiled. "I think it better that I do not answer that question, Leutnant. Suffice it to say that my destination is Lombez. The rest cannot be told."

"Ah," cried the young man, "now I understand. Security. Yes, Herr Oberst." He laughed before continuing. "In truth, sir, if you asked me the same question which I have just asked you, I would have to give the same answer. Security."

Holmes smiled. "Indeed, how so?" he said.

Von Richthofen grinned. "It is enough, sir, that if you examined army records you would find me listed as an officer attached to a communications unit in Belgium. My letters home indicate much the same thing ... and yet, here I am."

I found all this talk somewhat perplexing, partly because of my difficulty in understanding the German tongue, partly because the rush of wind past the open car made it very difficult to hear and partly because of the enigmatic tone of the conversation.

The journey in the motor car took less than an hour, and we were soon drawing to a halt outside a comfortable-looking inn near the centre of the village. With salutes and handshaking the young officer drove away and I, in my rôle of servant, carried the bags into the inn, Holmes walking a few yards ahead of me. The formalities over, we were soon ensconced, Holmes occupying a spacious suite on the second floor of the inn and I in an attic room in the servants' quarters. Nevertheless, it was far more prepossessing than the hut in which I had spent the previous night. A few minutes after settling in I went to Holmes's room, as a good servant would, to attend to my master. He was in one of his familiar moods of delight. "It's going along magnificently, Watson," he cried, rubbing his hands together in his enthusiasm. "That was a most fortuitous meeting on the road today."

"Well, yes," I agreed. "It certainly saved another long walk."

Holmes laughed. "No, more than that, much more. That young man, von Richthofen, is stationed here in Lombez at the army establishment nearby which is at this moment playing host to the Kaiser and his retinue."

"And how does that help us, Holmes?" My companion could at times be most obscure.

"Simply, Watson, that he has invited me to dine with him and his comrades in the officers' mess tonight. The Kaiser is to be guest of honour, and so it is not unlikely that I will be able to discover our agent there. We are nearing the end of the problem, old friend."

Holmes spent the afternoon out, returning about five o'clock. He had managed, from sources I could not imagine, to procure a German army colonel's full dress uniform, complete with appropriate decorations, and had also hired an open carriage and horse, which I was to drive that night. He had also acquired a great deal of information. "This is no ordinary army encampment, Watson," he explained urgently. "There is work going on here of the utmost secrecy, and it is concerned with aviation."

"Good Lord, Holmes," I cried. "But what relevance can that possibly have to our mission?"

"Just this," he replied. "If the Germans are engaged in something here, something that will harm the Allied cause, then it is up to us to discover just what it is, and if possible prevent it."

My heart sank. It seemed the period we were to spend behind enemy lines was getting longer and longer and the peril we faced more critical as the hours passed. Gloomily I nodded my agreement, and was rewarded by a hearty slap on the shoulders from Holmes. "Stout fellow," he said.

It was seven in the evening when we set out for the army establishment and the Kaiser's reception. My role was that of servant and coachman. It was no new thing for me to be driving a coach and horse, but there was the added incentive of remembering that the slightest mishap could cause the authorities to descend upon us, and with that a disastrous end to our secret mission.

We drove out for about two miles before arriving at the ornate gates marking the Château Lombez, which had given its name to the village as well as to the encampment. Sentries came rapidly to the alert as they caught sight of Holmes's impressive gold and grey uniform, and, after a word of explanation, they waved us through. In the manner of the best of coachmen I drove below the portico to the main entrance of the château and waited for the flunkies from the house to open the carriage door and let down the step so that Holmes could alight. I then took myself and the conveyance to an area some distance away which had been cordoned off for the vehicles to await the reappearance of their passengers.

A room had been set aside in one of the hastily erected army buildings where the drivers could await the return of their masters, and I was directed to this along with all the others. I considered waiting with the vehicle, but it became clear that as Holmes was to be away for several hours this would draw undue attention to our activities and put our plan in jeopardy. As soon as I entered the long, low, smoke-filled room my greatest fear became a reality. It was immediately apparent that conversation would be necessary, and with my lack of command of the German language that would mean instant discovery. A couple of maidservants had been detailed to serve tankards of a curious watery beer to the drivers, and as a question was put to me by one of the wenches I saw a possible avenue of avoiding detection. The girl had, of course, spoken in French, and I answered her in the same language. She did not mistake me for a Frenchman, but accepted my poor command of her language because she assumed I was German. If only I could seat myself with some French servants, then I could converse with them in my broken French.

I collected the beer and made my way between the tables. Before long I was struggling to hold a conversation in the French language with two elderly retainers who were now in service with the German occupying forces.

The evening wore on with little or no incident and I noticed that from time to time a name would be called out and that person would scurry away to attend to his master's needs. The elderly servant bellowing the names had called out "Schwarz" some three times before I realised it was I who was being addressed. I consulted my time-piece. It was something before eleven, and although I did not consider Holmes would yet have completed his business, I hurried to where our carriage was waiting. The area was deserted. There was no sign of Holmes, nor yet of anyone else, and I stamped around in the freezing cold. It was a clear, icy night and the lights from the chateau reflected eerily on the frosty ground. Faintly, through the tightly-barred windows, I could hear the strains of dance music.

Abruptly I was shaken by a voice close behind me. "Dr. Watson?" I turned, and found myself face to face with one of the loveliest women I had seen in my life. She was tall and slender, with a youthful countenance tinged with a hint of maturity and worldliness that placed her, had I been interested in so doing, in her early thirties. But my immediate concern was that here, in the heart of enemy territory, she had addressed me by my real name and in English.

She spoke again, and I noticed a lock of her flaxen hair had dislodged itself to fall against the cluster of black pearls at her throat. I stammered *"Nein, Fraulein,"* spreading wide my hands in surprise.

The woman laughed. "I really think you must be Doctor Watson," she said. "Although we have not met, I have already spoken this evening briefly with Mr. Holmes, and I understand that you are using the alias Schwarz."

There was nothing I could say. I simply gave a small bow and replied, in as gallant a fashion as I could muster, "At your service, Madam."

She laughed. "Good. Now we have that settled. I want you to deliver this for me." She handed me an envelope on which were inscribed the words, "Mr. Sherlock Holmes of Baker Street."

I took the envelope in some bewilderment, saying that I would do as she had bidden, and watched her as she returned to the ballroom.

It was only when the milk-white outline of her gown had disappeared into the gloom of the doorway that I noticed, on a second-storey balcony, another figure. It was a uniformed man, who had clearly been watching us closely. For a split second a light from the room behind caught his features and I recognised him. It was Leutnant von Richthofen.

"You are absolutely sure he was observing you?" asked Sherlock Holmes later. "It could not be that he had simply found the atmosphere at the reception oppressive and decided to take a breath of fresh air?"

I shook my head. "No, Holmes. He was watching us. I am sure he must suspect."

Holmes smiled, and, seating himself comfortably at one side of the fire in his temporary sitting room, began stuffing shag into the outsize bowl of his pipe. We had left the army encampment shortly after my mysterious meeting with the young woman, and this was the first opportunity we had had to discuss the surprising events of the evening

"Whether or not young Leutnant von Richthofen was watching you, Watson," said Holmes, "we may not have to worry overlong about him. I am sure that soon we shall be on our way back to England."

"You mean that you have managed to contact the British agent so soon?" I cried in amazement.

"It was really no problem," said my companion modestly. "In London Mycroft was unwilling to tell me the identity of his agent, since he did not think I would need to know. Yet once I saw the Kaiser's retinue, that identity was immediately apparent."

"You mean you recognised him instantly, Holmes?" I queried. "How can that be?"

Sherlock Holmes ripped open the envelope I had been handed. The message was simple and brief: 'Remain at the inn tomorrow. I will call on you. Nina'.

"Nina," I cried. "Then this agent is a woman - is Nina Vassilievna? It was she who sought me out this evening?"

"Quite right, Watson," said Holmes, chuckling at my surprise. "It is indeed the daughter of my old friend Irene Adler, she whom I last met at the Tsar's court in Russia when I was involved in that business of the explosive[1].

"You will recall that she was brought up in Bohemia by the ruling family, and although she was introduced into the court of the Tsar by

1 Sherlock Holmes and the earthquake machine

the man she called Uncle Willie, the King of Bohemia, she was even at that time a correspondent of the British Government and an agent of Mycroft's department in particular. She is clearly still pursuing her career as a secret agent, and where more obvious to station her than at the court of the Kaiser - she was, after all, brought up by the ruling family of one of the provinces of his country. With luck we shall be able to alert her to the danger now facing her, and plan our escape tomorrow. In a couple of days we should all be back in England."

"That is excellent news, Holmes," I said with feeling. "I trust everything will go well from now on. But I must confess to slight unease as far as that young officer is concerned."

"You mean Leutnant Manfred von Richthofen? I agree, Watson, he is as dangerous as a rattlesnake. He is twenty-three years old and has spent his entire life in military surroundings. He was enrolled as a cadet at the age of eleven and became an officer in 1911 with a crack light cavalry regiment In the early weeks of the war he served on the Eastern front with his regiment and was decorated with the Iron Cross."

"He has a distinguished record," I remarked. "But many soldiers have that, even so young. Where is the especial danger?"

Holmes shook his head. "The danger, Watson, lies in his present rôle and what he might do. A couple of months ago he was transferred from his regiment to a unit in Belgium called *Brieftauben Abteilung*. Translated, that means Carrier Pigeon Section, but in truth it is a secret experimental aviation unit. He is, however, also very active in this secret establishment here. Caution must be our watchword, Watson."

We were interrupted by a gentle tap at the door At a gesture from Holmes, I stepped smartly across, once again adopting my pose as exemplar German soldier servant, and opened it. It was the landlord of the inn. In his fractured German the old Frenchman apologised profusely for the lateness of the hour, but said there was a visitor for the Herr Oberst. For a moment it baffled me, but the old man, with nods of the head in the direction of Holmes, eventually made me understand. A visitor for Holmes, at one in the morning! The old man pushed a small rectangle of pasteboard into my hand. I looked at it briefly and without a word handed it to Sherlock Holmes.

The card read: 'Leutnant Manfred Freiherr von Richthofen'.

The giant 'plane

"An odd time to come calling," remarked Holmes coolly, as he read the card. "He had better come up, Watson."

A few moments later Leutnant von Richthofen was ushered into Holmes's sitting-room. The visitor was not alone. He had brought with him another man, middle-aged and heavily built, with cropped, steel-grey hair and an old duelling scar on his right cheek.

Von Richthofen stood smartly to attention. "Herr Oberst," he addressed Holmes, "please forgive the lateness of the visit and permit me to present Count Hantelmann."

Holmes gave a sharp military bow in the direction of the count and waved the men to chairs. "I am honoured to meet the count," he said. "And as to the lateness of the hour, it is of no importance. We are, after all, at war. The usual conventions need not apply."

At Holmes's instructions I fetched brandy and glasses for the guests, and soon the atmosphere in the room became heavily charged, spirit fumes mingling with the aroma of cigars provided by the count. But beneath the air of bonhomie lurked a tension difficult to ignore. As I stood rigidly next to the sideboard, ready to replenish the glasses, concentrated on following the conversation while at the same time reassuring myself that my pistol was loaded and ready to hand. It was a remark from the count which put me most on my guard.

"I had heard, Schumacher," he said to Holmes, "that you were dead - lost in action."

My friend coolly exhaled a spiral of smoke from his cigar. "The report was somewhat exaggerated my dear Count," he replied with a degree of equanimity.

"Nevertheless, it must be a remarkable story?" the Count persisted.

Holmes waved a deprecating hand. "No, it is a common enough occurrence at the front. A man is advancing or patrolling in No Man's Land, there is a shell-burst and the man is gone. His comrades report him missing and eyewitnesses testify they saw him blown up. Some time later the man, who was indeed blown up, awakens to find himself alone in No Man's Land, with a headache from the shell-burst, but no other injury. He is then either taken prisoner by the enemy, and escapes or not as the case may be - or, if fortunate, he is not captured and makes his own way back to his comrades. I assure you that it is nothing remarkable," Holmes continued. "It happens to many men. Why, I believe young von Richthofen here had a similar adventure not long ago. Did you not tell me so this evening, Leutnant?"

The young officer nodded. "Yes, it is just so. I was in Russia in a skirmish with some Cossacks. I was missing for some few days. My mother had already received visits of condolence."

The Count smiled. "Then we must congratulate you, Schumacher, on your escape. Tell me, are you remaining long in Lombez?"

Holmes paused before speaking. "Really, Count, I cannot divulge my mission even to you. You must understand."

"Of course, my dear fellow, of course." Count Hantelmann rose to his feet. "But I trust we can have your company at dinner before you leave. I am staying at the château. And now, since the hour is so late, I think we must leave. It has been pleasant, Herr Oberst."

I thought I detected the slightest emphasis on the last two words as I brought the two Germans their greatcoats, but Sherlock Holmes gave no indication of noticing anything wrong. In his guise of the German colonel he blandly bade farewell to his guests before returning to the sitting-room.

"Watson, I think things are beginning to warm up a little," he said. "Are you aware of the identity of our distinguished visitor?"

I shook my head. "You mean the Count? No. Some friend of von Richthofen's, I suppose."

Sherlock Holmes gave a grim smile. "Count Hantelmann is the chief of Germany's *Sicherheitspolizei*. Security police. I have heard of him before, Watson. He is reputed to be an expert in the torture chamber; a brutal employer of scoundrels and rogues to further his own ends. He is one of the vilest, most powerful and least known men in Germany. I should also think that in wartime he is one of the busiest - yet he finds time to come visiting here."

I started. "Good Heavens, Holmes, you don't think they could possibly suspect us, do you?"

Sherlock Holmes gazed steadily from his chair on the opposite side of the dying fire in the grate. "Of course they suspect. What else could bring the most feared man in Germany to the door of our inn at this time of night? Here I am, assuming the identity of a German regular soldier who is reported dead. I turn up at a secret establishment and refuse to explain myself. What could they do but suspect? Hantelmann realises that I am not Schumacher. Consequently, he also knows that you are not a real German soldier. If we have adopted the identities of dead Germans, then it is clear to Hantelmann that we must be spies. He is now waiting to see what we are up to."

Suddenly the room felt cold, and I threw another log on the fire. "It's a desperate game we are playing, Holmes," I remarked. "More perilous than any in the past."

"You are right, Watson. Would that you had not joined me in this venture, old friend. They are on to us very quickly. The only answer is for us to be even quicker." He paused. "We shall wait for Nina Vassilievna tomorrow, and then ... England." Holmes's tone brightened as he spoke these words, but I doubted whether we would see home again. We were alone in enemy territory, suspected of spying and watched by security police. In my view there could be but one end to this escapade. I left Holmes gazing into the fire and went to my room.

I slept fitfully, and shortly after dawn returned downstairs, where I found Holmes still in the same armchair amid a cloud of stale pipe smoke.

It was shortly after breakfast had been brought up that the innkeeper nervously tapped at the door "A lady to see you, Colonel," he announced, and was then unceremoniously brushed aside as the woman I now recognised as Nina Vassilievna strode into the room.

She thrust out her hand and pumped furiously at my companion's arm. "Sherlock," she cried "Here, of all places. It is a delight to see you, my dear." So saying, she threw her arms round Holmes's neck and planted kisses, in the continental fashion, upon both his cheeks.

My friend, somewhat embarrassedly, I thought, disentangled himself from this brash display of affection and turned in my direction. "You must allow me to present Doctor Watson," he said. Gingerly, I held out my hand. Nina Vassilievna, now elegantly attired in a day dress of red velvet, gently clasped my fingers and smiled. "When last I met Sherlock Holmes, you occupied a great deal of our conversation," she said flatteringly. Abruptly she turned back to Holmes. "But you must tell me now. Why are you here?"

"Because, Nina, you are in the gravest peril." Sherlock Holmes spoke sharply. "You must return to London with Dr. Watson and myself."

"Pah! I am always in grave danger," exclaimed the girl. "Was I not in grave danger all the time I was in Russia? Now I am in danger from the Germans. This is nothing. It is my business to be in danger."

"You are almost certain to be exposed as a British spy if you remain here," said Holmes, and he went on briefly to explain the events which had taken place since the escape of Von Bork from the Tower of London. "You must understand that it is very possible that some sort of message was received at the Kaiser's headquarters from Herr Lubin that evening, before he killed himself on my arrival."

Nina Vassilievna sat down. "It is impossible for me to leave now. I have information concerning two major projects which the Germans have in hand. Projects that could change the course of the war. It is essential that two things happen. First that you take messages back to England for me and second, that I remain here to finish my work. If I fail, you will have reported my progress thus far: if I succeed, a great blow will have been struck at the German war effort."

Sherlock Holmes poured coffee from the pot which had been brought earlier. "You may possibly be correct. However, before making a decision I think you should tell us what it is you have discovered."

We settled in armchairs and Nina Vassilievna began her story. "The first critically important piece of information concerns an attempt to assassinate Asquith, Kitchener and other members of the War Cabinet."

"Good Lord," I expostulated. "Assassination? We are supposed to be civilised countries. Surely they would never do such a thing?"

"I am afraid they will, Doctor," replied Nina. "The Kaiser resisted the plan for a long time. He, like you, found assassination a despicable weapon. But when the war became something of a stalemate his attitude changed. Hantelmann was able to convince him that by killing a dozen or so men he would shorten the war by years and save thousands of German lives. He was reluctant, but finally agreed."

"But how are they to carry out this plan?" Sherlock Holmes leaned forward in his chair as he rekindled his pipe.

Nina Vassilievna shrugged. "The details are top secret. I am unable to discover them. But this much I do know so far. The plan involved landing a large group of agents on the east coast of England, at a village somewhere near the garrison town of Colchester. They are already there."

"Heaven's Portal," breathed Sherlock Holmes.

"Good Lord," I interjected.

"Yes," cried Nina Vassilievna, "that is the very place. There is a large country house there. It is to be used as a permanent base by the agents in England. From there they can carry out a programme of assassination of national leaders, sabotage of naval and military installations and the gathering of intelligence. It is vital that this information gets back to London, Mr. Holmes; you must see that."

Holmes nodded. "This, of course, accounts for Von Bork's dallying under the fire of the Navy until he was able to reach Heaven's Portal. The information must reach Mycroft as soon as possible, and arrests must take place immediately. That is serious enough, but what of the second ploy?"

"Ah! That, too, is desperately dangerous for the British." Nina paused and looked somewhat unhappily at the tepid coffee before her. She turned to me. "Don't you have brandy?" she enquired.

Although it was still five minutes short of eleven o'clock, I brought a bottle of brandy from the sideboard and poured three goblets. The intrepid young lady took a deep draught, then continued speaking. "There is not far from here a flying field. It has been established in the last few months and is very secret. Naturally, the Germans cannot expect to conceal the existence of such a place, and they have based a number of scout planes there. These pilots occasionally fly over the British lines, and the airfield is to all intents and purposes an ordinary support unit. But it has a more sinister purpose. It is here that all research into matters concerned with aviation is now taking place. They have brought inventors and scientists from all over Germany. Young pilots have been drafted from all areas to help in testing the machines. Mr. Holmes, they are close to perfecting two deadly weapons for use in the air."

Holmes and I were both leaning forward in our chairs as Nina Vassilievna continued her chilling narrative. "They have built a machine-gun which will fire between the blades of an aircraft propeller," she announced.

I was a little mystified as to the significance of this. "But how can that be of use?" I asked.

"It means that the pilot of a single-seat scout plane will have a fixed gun in front of him. He will be able to line up his aircraft and shoot any other plane out of the sky. At present pilots use all types of weapons -

rifles, pistols, portable machine-guns. But even worse than that, they have built a prototype aircraft to carry the weapon. It is a single-wing aircraft, a monoplane, constructed of metal, and has enormous speed, strength and manœuvrability. It will give the Germans complete mastery of the air over the trenches."

Holmes spoke grimly. "There is little point in merely destroying this prototype, which doubtless we could do with little trouble. There will be plans, and the Germans would proceed to construct a second. No, rather we must take the plans, or indeed, the plane itself, to negate any advantage the enemy have. London must not lag behind events: Mycroft must know of these developments."

Nina Vassilievna nodded uncertainly. "To steal the design drawings of a top secret aircraft and its armament is not going to be easy, even for me."

"I agree," said Holmes. "It must, however, be done. And the second deadly weapon you spoke of?"

"Yes," she replied. "And the difficulties are much the same, although perhaps this is not such a desperate matter. The scientists here are working on a second type of aircraft. They are calling it the *Riesenflugzeug*, or the giant plane. It has four engines, two placed on each wing, and it can carry as many bombs as a Zeppelin. It has a crew of six men and a range which will take it easily to London and back. They call it the 'flying elephant,' it is so big, and yet its speed is almost as great as a single-seater scout plane."

I gasped. "Why, with this aircraft the Germans will be invincible. They will be able to drop bombs on our cities with impunity. And the other aircraft you mention, why, that will mean the enemy dominates the Western Front. They will be able to strafe our trenches at will."

"Yes, Doctor," the girl agreed, "and not only the Western Front, they will have complete mastery. The air of Europe will belong to the Kaiser. His aeroplanes will pound the Allies into defeat in weeks. If he manages to destroy the leaders of the British war effort and to acquire these terrible new weapons, the result of the war will be a foregone conclusion."

Sherlock Holmes broke into the conversation. "I am a little intrigued," he said, "as to why the Kaiser has decided to situate this establishment here, in occupied territory? Surely from the German point of view it would be safer deep inside Germany itself?"

"Perhaps," said Nina. "But with the British air raids on installations in Germany, they have decided to put this secret airfield here. After all, what could be better? It is safely away from the area of fighting, but near enough that the comings and goings of soldiers and aircraft cause no curiosity. Don't forget that the British have been raiding Zeppelin sheds for three months now, and those sheds are deep in Germany. We heard only yesterday that Royal Navy seaplanes attacked the Zeppelin sheds at Cuxhaven on the estuary of the Elbe on Christmas Day. They have also attacked similar establishments at Düsseldorf, Cologne and Friedrichshaven recently. It is no secret that the British regard the Zeppelin as the greatest threat to the security of England. If they were to hear of these two new aircraft and the new machine-gun, the assumption would be made that they were in Germany. If they are situated here in occupied French territory, the Kaiser thinks he can keep them secret."

"Yes, but now that we have the secret, those raids can take place," I spoke quickly. "The Royal Flying Corps and the Royal Naval Air Service will be able to take care of this place in an afternoon."

Sherlock Holmes chuckled. "It is not so easy, Watson. I am certain that our own fliers could delay production and development of these devices sufficiently to inconvenience the Kaiser, but no more than that. Most importantly, we have to make sure that our people are not lagging behind in this research. Nina is quite correct. We must have the plans."

"But," I protested, "that would mean leaving Nina behind, here in enemy territory. We cannot do that, Holmes. You know that she is almost certain to be discovered."

Nina spoke. "But what else can we do? Besides, as I have already said, I am no stranger to perilous missions."

Sherlock Holmes struck yet another match, lighting the handful of shag he had been stuffing into the bowl of his pipe. "There is, of course, the other possibility," he said. "If we cannot have the plans, we must have the aircraft."

Nina Vassilievna and I both stared at him in astonishment. "Surely you are not serious?" I cried.

"Well," he said, "do you think we could kidnap a pilot?"

"That would not be necessary," said the girl slowly. "I can fly an aircraft as well as any pilot, and I could instruct you in the art of flying."

"Then I shall take the single-seater with the machine-gun," said Sherlock Holmes, "and you will fly the giant plane with Watson as your crew."

"Really, Holmes," I cried. "Enough of this madness. You have never flown an aeroplane in your life. You will kill yourself!"

Thoughtfully, Nina Vassilievna spoke. "It is possible: to fly the monoplane is not so difficult. If there is time enough for you to learn, we may manage it. But there are further difficulties. It is not so easy to steal an aeroplane and fly with it to freedom. First, we have to take possession of the aircraft; then there will be others chasing us - the Germans have a flight of pursuit planes stationed at this airfield. It will not be a picnic."

"I don't expect a picnic," said Sherlock Holmes, "I expect a lesson in the art of driving an aeroplane."

An Interview with the Kaiser

The next few hours were spent with Nina instructing Sherlock Holmes in the art of flying an aeroplane; by three in the afternoon she pronounced him as knowledgeable as he could be without actually sitting in the cockpit and said that it was time to leave. Darkness fell shortly before five o'clock and our task was timed so that we should have taken the aircraft and be on our way while there was still an hour of daylight. There was a slight delay while our companion disappeared into a small shop adjoining the inn.

"Really, Holmes," I protested, "don't you think she could have found a more appropriate time to do her shopping?"

Holmes smiled. "I am sure there is some reason," he remarked as the young woman emerged. To my utter astonishment she was clad in a short jacket and breeches. I hastily looked in another direction as she approached the motor car in which Holmes and I were already seated. "I rarely feel comfortable in petticoats," she said, climbing into the driving seat of the vehicle, "especially when I am engaged in an exploit such as this." How the world was changing, I reflected.

It was a journey of a few minutes to reach the airfield, a flat expanse of grassland with some long, low sheds at one end and a number of small aeroplanes dotted hither and thither. A few casually-dressed men lounged about, but there was none of the strict military security one would have expected to see at an establishment as secret as this.

"Oh, it is quite normal," replied Nina in response to a question from Holmes, who was apparently thinking along the same lines. "Those men whom you see are well able to deal with any problem that might arise."

We drove to one of the sheds and Nina drove the motor car close to it. As we descended I saw to my dismay a German sergeant in the Air Service approaching. To my relief he gave Nina Vassilievna a cheery greeting. "Are you going up today, *Fraulein*?" he called.

Nina shook her head. "No, not today, Heinrich," she replied with a smile. She waved a hand towards Holmes and myself. "I'm just showing some visitors around."

We entered the shed, an enormous building despite its low roof, and there in front of us stood three aeroplanes. Two were clearly the all-metal single-seaters which Nina Vassilievna had described earlier. The third was without doubt the Giant Plane.

"You can see why the pilots call it the 'flying elephant,'" laughed Nina, gesturing towards the belly of the aircraft. "But let us look at the single seater."

She and Holmes climbed on to the wing of one of the monoplanes and leaned over the cockpit as she began to explain the controls. "Here is the throttle on the right," she said, "and here on the dashboard you will find a fuel gauge. You see, the plane has full tanks at the moment."

"Then I shall shortly have a chance to convert the theory of aeroplane driving into practice," said Holmes.

From a few yards behind, a harsh voice interrupted us. "I do not think so, Mr. Sherlock Holmes. You are not going anywhere - for all three of you, the war is over."

Turning, I saw to my horror that the speaker was the sinister Count Hantelmann. Standing beside him, a heavy automatic pistol trained in our direction, was the young officer, von Richthofen, and ranged across the aircraft shed, their rifles at the ready, were a dozen infantrymen.

We all three raised our hands above our heads. The Count smiled. "Good, and now, if you would just come away from that aeroplane, I should be much obliged."

"It appears that you have me at something of a disadvantage, Count," said Sherlock Holmes, leaping to the ground, his hands still above his head.

"That is so," replied Hantelmann. "You have been at a considerable disadvantage ever since you arrived here. I have been expecting you."

Sherlock Holmes sighed. "Then Von Bork's message did get through," he said.

"Yes, Mr. Holmes, it did," replied Hantelmann. "All except for one vital piece of information. The agent sending the message from Paris was interrupted before he could give me the identity of the spy here. But, knowing that you were on the way, I simply decided to wait. You did exactly as I had hoped and led me to your agent, whom I was disconcerted to find was this delightful young lady. Now, you will answer some rather pertinent questions for us before we shoot you."

"I regret that I shall be unable to help you, my dear Count," said Sherlock Holmes. "I am here to collect information, not to impart it."

"In that case," replied the Count, "we shall have a great deal of amusement with you ... particularly with little Nina here." His hand swung towards the lady, and for an instant I saw the gleam of a heavy ring. Hantelmann's hand caught Nina Vassilievna on the right side of her face, leaving a long gash.

"You scoundrel," I cried when I perceived what he had done, and without thought for my own safety I leapt towards him. As I did so I was clubbed to the ground by a heavy blow to my head.

I regained consciousness lying on a stone floor, my head cushioned on a jacket and Sherlock Holmes leaning anxiously over me. "Are you all right, Watson?" he was asking.

Despite the violent throbbing in my head I gave him the assurances he wanted. "I am recovered now, Holmes," I said ruefully.

"That was a deuce of a crack he gave you," said Holmes. "It was one of the soldiers when you lunged towards Hantelmann - he struck you with his rifle butt."

I looked around me at windowless stone walls. "Where are we, Holmes?" I asked. "And where is Nina?"

"We are in the dungeons below the Château Lombez," replied Holmes, "and Nina Vassilievna has been lodged just along the corridor. They brought us back here while you were still unconscious."

I started to climb to my feet, but a wave of nausea swept over me and Holmes gently but insistently made me lie back. "You will be better off lying here for a while, Watson," he said. "A rifle butt can cause a serious injury. You are doubtless concussed."

Lying on the stone floor, I began to reflect on the hopelessness of our position. We had failed. Now there was only the prospect of the brutalities of an interrogation by Hantelmann, followed by the firing squad. Eventually I fell into a fitful sleep, awakening later as the door of our cell crashed open. Hantelmann stood there. "On your feet," he rasped. "You are about to be honoured."

His men manhandled us out of the cell and up numerous flights of stairs until we reached what was apparently the ground floor of the château. I was surprised to see light streaming through the windows, and realised we had spent the whole of the night in the foul cell far below. We were led along wide corridors and then pushed through a set of tall double doors.

"Bow to the Emperor," snarled Hantelmann, and to my surprise I found myself face to face with the familiar features of Kaiser William II, Emperor of Germany. I saw that Nina Vassilievna was already in the room.

We stood, the three of us, lined up in front of a table at which the Emperor and several other people were seated. Away to our right there was another small group, some in uniform, some quite elderly. The Kaiser, clearly recognisable from his upturned moustaches and withered arm, spoke in English.

''You are Mr. Sherlock Holmes?"

My friend bowed. "I am, sir," he replied.

"It is a great honour to meet you," said the Kaiser. "I have read of your exploits, of course," and here he gave a nod in my direction. The voice trailed away, and he seemed to be distracted by something. Then he took a grip of himself, and spoke again. "Why are you in our territory, Mr. Holmes?"

"With respect, Sir," began Sherlock Holmes "we are at present in France, a country allied to my own."

"Come, come, man, don't bandy words with me. Why are you here?" A note of anger crept into the Kaiser's voice.

Holmes replied coldly. "A mission of some delicacy. More than that, I will not say."

William regarded Sherlock Holmes for several long seconds. "Surely you do not think that you can just walk away from here, now that you are discovered? You are lost, man. You can do no more. There is nothing left for you but the firing squad. On the other hand, if you cooperate with my officers, you and your companions will escape a great deal of suffering, and may even preserve your lives."

Holmes stood rigidly before the Emperor. "I cannot give your people any aid at all, Sir. Our countries are at war. Whatever the cost to myself, and unhappily to my friends also, I cannot buy our comfort or our freedom at the expense of my honour."

The Kaiser appeared nonplussed. "But surely ... you ... we are both civilised ..." As had happened a few moments before, his voice trailed off, his concentration apparently completely lost, and my medical training told me that this all-powerful monarch was a very sick man. Stories of the Crown Prince, his son, taking an increasingly active part in the conduct of the war seemed to have the stamp of truth.

But an aide was reminding the Kaiser of the purpose of the meeting, and with an effort he again pulled himself together. "You would see your comrade, Dr. Watson, suffer because of your stubbornness, Mr. Holmes?" said he. Another effort. "And young Nina? What of her? Would you condemn her also?"

Sherlock Holmes spoke clearly. "I would condemn no one, Sir. That is a matter for you. I must hold to the position I have previously stated."

The Kaiser rose unsteadily from his chair and walked round the table. He stopped by Nina Vassilievna. "Surely, child, you are not going to be as unhelpful as Mr. Holmes? You will tell Count Hantelmann what he wants to know, won't you?" He placed an arm round her shoulders.

Nina shrugged off the Kaiser's friendly gesture, and a shake of her head conveyed her answer.

"But Nina," wheedled the monarch. "Come, come, we must be sensible. What would your Uncle Willie say if he knew you were behaving in such an unhelpful manner? He would be very unhappy, you know."

"He is dead," said Nina Vassilievna. "Whatever allegiance I owe to him and to Bohemia does not extend to you and your domain. It especially does not extend to your effort in this bloody war. I have nothing to say."

"Please do not try to make me cross, Nina," said the elderly man. "I remember that as a child you were fond of baiting your elders. I want you to be sensible so that I can help you."

Nina spat out an obscene phrase full in the face of the Kaiser, causing him to recoil in horror and drawing gasps from the other people in the room.

The Kaiser went back to his chair. "Then there is nothing I can do for any of you. Hantelmann! You are to investigate fully the activities of these people, discover who has aided them and what they want here. When you have completed the interrogation, you may do with them as you will. Take them out."

As we turned towards the door an elderly man who was traversing the room collided with Holmes. I saw a glance pass between them, and then the three of us were hustled from the room by Hantelmann and his cronies and led back to the bowels of the château.

We were thrown into our cells and once more left alone. I turned to Holmes. "Who was that old man?"

"He was the Count von und zu Grafenstein. We met briefly in the winter of '06," said Sherlock Holmes.

"Of course," I exclaimed, "it was he and his family who were on a state visit to St. Petersburg while you were hunting anarchists there."

"That is so, anarchists and worse. The Count there was riding with the Tsar when a nihilist hurled a bomb. Fortunately I was on the spot and was able to extinguish the fuse. Nina Vassilievna was there too. She was in the Tsar's court then, but that will help us little now."

Gloomily I agreed, and settled down to rest since my head was still aching from the blow I had received. Later in the day Holmes and I were dragged into Hantelmann's interrogation room and asked a number of questions relating to our movements since crossing the lines. The brutality I had expected did not materialise and, towards the end of the afternoon, we were taken back to our cell and given a meal of cabbage soup and black bread.

Holmes addressed himself to the poor fare with a will, for we had not eaten since we were arrested.

"The interrogation was quite easy to stand," I remarked as we ate.

"So far, Watson," said Holmes coolly.

The long hours passed slowly. My timepiece told me it was just before dawn when I was awakened by a key turning in the lock of our cell door. Holmes and I jumped to our feet at the same instant. The door opened and in came the elderly man we had seen the previous day, the Count von und zu Grafenstein. Hurriedly he pushed the door to behind him.

"Mr. Holmes," he began in conspiratorial tones, "some eight years ago in St. Petersburg you prevented the nihilist Klopman from killing myself and my wife. I was able to thank you at the time, but it is a matter of honour that since that day I am in your debt. My family and I owe you our lives. Fate has now decreed that I am in a position to repay you, and as a matter of honour I must do so. Although you are an enemy of my country, it is my duty to free you."

"Thank you, sir," Holmes spoke crisply. "And Nina Vassilievna?"

"We will free her now. Come, it will seem as though you are in my custody."

We followed the bent figure along the stone corridor, passing a number of guards who leaped to attention, and, selecting a key from a ring he held in his hand, Grafenstein opened the door of a cell. Nina Vassilievna, dishevelled and unkempt, blinked as light flooded the squalid room.

"Nina, quickly," Holmes beckoned urgently, and the girl joined us at once. The old count led us up a series of staircases until we arrived at a heavy oak door.

"This is a side door to the château grounds," whispered the count. "You are still in German uniform, so if you let yourselves out here and walk smartly out of the grounds, you are unlikely to be detained. Go now. There is nothing more I can do for you. Godspeed." So saying, the old man went back along the corridor and disappeared into a side room.

We stood for a moment, each savouring the good fortune which had brought about our release. Then Nina spoke. "Well, it's a long way to London, even by plane. We had better press ahead."

I smiled, and tugged the door open. The smile died on my lips. I was face to face with Leutnant von Richthofen.

"Mr. Holmes is Dead!"

The Leutnant was shocked into immobility by our appearance. He had clearly been about to enter the château when suddenly he found himself facing the three prisoners he had helped to capture. I was conscious of a rapid movement to my left, and realised that it was Sherlock Holmes lunging forward to reach the young officer. In a split second the skirmish was over. A single blow from Holmes had laid von Richthofen at our feet.

"Quickly, help me, Watson." Holmes bent to the task of tying up our prisoner with his own belt and gagging him with a handkerchief. I relieved von Richthofen of the automatic pistol he carried.

Fearing discovery at any moment, we dashed to the front of the château, where vehicles were habitually left. A motor car was standing there unattended and after two swings on the starting-handle the engine burst into life. Seconds later we were driving towards the airfield.

Dawn was just breaking as we arrived. We drove straight to the sheds housing the aircraft and, leaving Nina Vassilievna to keep guard outside, Holmes and I entered. There was a solitary armed guard dozing near the 'flying elephant'. I took a rapid pace towards him and slammed the butt of my pistol against the side of his head. He collapsed without a sound and I caught his rifle, tossing it to Holmes. We called Nina and quickly checked that the ammunition drums on the guns were loaded.

We dragged open the huge doors at the front of the shed and prepared ourselves for the journey. "My God," cried Nina Vassilievna. In the distance we could see a small convoy of motor lorries bumping along the road to the airfield. "That must be Hantelmann and von Richthofen. How on earth can they be so close behind us? Quickly!"

Holmes hastily climbed into the cockpit of the monoplane and, as Nina swung the propeller, the engine fired and he was off. As the plane bumped across the grass field I heard a spatter of rifle fire. The Germans were getting closer.

Nina took her seat at the controls of the 'flying elephant'. At her signal I swung each of the four propellers in turn, and then jumped into the open door in the belly of the plane. I was unable to see anything of what was happening, but I noticed a gunport, equipped with a machine-gun, above my head. I stood on a ledge and put my head through the hole, finding myself looking out of the top of the body of the great aeroplane. Despite my total inexperience in such surroundings, I seized the gun that was in front of me, threw off the safety catch and gave a number of short bursts towards the group of soldiers firing at us. As they scattered for cover I felt the plane lurch upwards, and knew that we were flying. Going forward to the pilot's cabin I took the seat adjacent to Nina's. The noise of the engines was tremendous and I was unable to hear her speak, but she handed me a leather helmet to which was attached a form of telephone apparatus which made conversation possible, while at the same time it deadened the noise from the four petrol engines.

"Look there, Doctor." She pointed ahead. "There is Sherlock Holmes."

I squinted into the early morning light, and could just see a silver speck far ahead. Looking over my shoulder I saw several similar specks in the sky. "Are you sure he is not over there?" I asked, pointing.

Nina Vassilievna followed the direction of my arm. She pulled a grim face and shook her head. "No, Doctor, Sherlock Holmes is not there, he is well ahead. What you see there is Leutnant von Richthofen's pursuit squadron."

Minutes later the air was buzzing with the angry sound of the engines of the scout planes which had been sent in pursuit of us. Von Richthofen was clearly visible as he flew alongside us in the second of the prototype monoplanes. Leaning over the side of his cockpit he pointed downwards. There was no mistaking his meaning: he wanted us to return to the airfield, and, making it clear that there was no alternative, he fired a short burst from his guns across our bows.

I looked at Nina. "We are going to have to fight," she said. "But there are at least four of them - we must even the odds as quickly as possible. I will gain height; when von Richthofen is out of sight, you go back and man the machine-guns. When he climbs back to his position alongside you can rake him with gunfire."

She pulled back on the control stick, and immediately our aeroplane surged upwards, leaving von Richthofen far below. Rapidly I clambered back into the body of the plane and once again found the gunner's position. Cautiously I poked my head through the trap door and checked the ammunition drums again: I had not been able to gauge the number of rounds I had used as we took off, but happily all was well.

As Nina Vassilievna had predicted, von Richthofen's aircraft quickly followed our climb, and as he pulled abreast once more I squinted along the sights and squeezed the trigger. To my surprise my shots went wide. Although I had had the cockpit and engine of his plane square in my sights most of my shots missed, and the few that did connect were far to the rear of the plane, leaving a line of black dots on the fuselage. I realised I had failed to make sufficient allowance for deflection while shooting at a rapidly moving target, and set myself the task once more of shooting down von Richthofen.

But I was not to have the chance. In the second that I started firing von Richthofen threw his controls over and the plane dived away below us, falling momentarily out of my range of vision. Then suddenly the sky was alive with attacking aircraft. Von Richthofen came again from below, immediately distinguishable in his monoplane, accompanied by three biplanes from the pursuit squadron. They came at us from all directions and I could hear bullets plopping through the canvas skin of the giant plane. The shriek of bullets striking our metal engine-casing caused me to glance upward, and I saw one of the biplanes, guns blazing, falling down towards us at a tremendous speed. I jerked up my machine-gun and returned the fire, holding it in the sights for more than ten seconds as I poured round after round into the tiny aircraft. Still he plunged towards us and I could clearly discern the pilot. He was slumped over his controls, either dead or unconscious. As he hurtled past I saw small flames and wreaths of smoke leaping from the engine of his craft. Suddenly the plane dissolved into an orange ball of incandescence, the force of the explosion jarring our giant aircraft and slewing it round in the sky.

Two more aircraft were diving towards the rear of our plane and, as tracer shells ripped into the fuselage, I caught a glimpse of the silver plane of von Richthofen coming in from the forward quarter. I swivelled my gun, firing bursts alternately at the two attackers to the rear and von Richthofen ahead. I could hear the sound of bullets striking the wire rigging, and for a moment lost my balance as our plane went into a steep dive, leaving all our attackers above and behind us.

Nina's voice came in my ear. "We have a problem, Doctor Watson. One engine has stopped and another is losing power. We may be forced down."

I stole a glance at the engines. On the port wing one propeller was stationary. To starboard another engine was firing only intermittently. Both had clearly been struck by bullets during the attack. But I had no time to consider the problem further, for von Richthofen and his two companions were once more pouring fire into our aircraft. Hastily I clipped in a further drum of ammunition, and threw yet another shield of automatic fire as the 'planes plunged towards us. From the corner of my eye I saw the outer engine on the starboard side had now completely stopped.

"It's no good, Doctor," cried Nina Vassilievna over our telephone link, "I can hardly keep her from going down. We must gain more height."

Only two aircraft made the next attack, and as I was returning their fire I realised that von Richthofen was flying below us and shooting into the under-belly of our plane. There was nothing I could do. A shot from our attackers ricochetted from one of the wing struts and embedded itself in the breech of my machine-gun, instantly putting it out of action. We were helpless.

Then, from far above, I saw a silver monoplane hurtling down, its guns blazing. Von Richthofen. I thought, he must have climbed rapidly. Unable to return his fire, I could only watch in horror as the plane plunged towards us. A vast shock wave hammered at the 'flying elephant' as one of the attacking biplanes disintegrated in a vast explosion. For a moment, I was perplexed, for I had taken no part in shooting at it. Then, as the silver monoplane dived past us, I could clearly see its pilot.

"It is Holmes!" I cried in relief. "He has returned to assist us."

"Just as well," came the dour reply from Nina Vassilievna. "This cow of an aeroplane is not going to stay up much longer."

Von Richthofen and his one remaining comrade had broken off the attack upon us as Holmes hurtled between them, firing first at one and then the other, diving and soaring, looping and spinning. I watched the progress of the fight from my gunnery position. Nina managed to gain a little height, despite the poor condition of our machine, and soon the aerial battle was two or three miles distant.

"Could we not assist Holmes?" I asked.

"What can we do?" The girl's voice was stern in my ear. "Our aircraft is disabled and scarcely able to fly. Our guns are out of action. We would not even be able to catch up with them. We would be nothing more than a target. Besides, it is essential that we get over the lines with our information."

She was right, of course. There was nothing we could do. Helplessly I watched Sherlock Holmes gamely trying to attack his two adversaries. As we drew further away I could see lines of tracer shells flickering between the different craft, but now I was unable to distinguish between the almost identical planes of Holmes and von Richthofen.

"We are passing over the lines now," said Nina Vassilievna. "I shall look for a place to land."

I glanced down and saw the trench systems spread out below me, columns of men here and there scurrying about like ants. I tore my gaze away and looked back to the air battle: to my horror, I saw one of the monoplanes in a desperate dive, slewing from side to side, trying to avoid the murderous stream of bullets coming from its two pursuers. Much as it twisted and turned, both attackers stayed relentlessly behind the silver monoplane. I last saw all three diving into a bank of cloud. A while later two aircraft emerged and circled triumphantly above the cloud for a moment, then wheeled in our direction and again took up the chase.

"They are after us once more," I said, and paused. "I think Holmes went down."

"Oh." Nina Vassilievna was silent. Then she spoke again. "I can see an airfield. Be careful, Doctor; we are liable to be at risk whether it is an Allied or German field."

The two German planes, seeing they would not reach us before we landed, dived back towards their own base, and a few minutes later our plane was bumping across the uneven grass of a British airfield.

We drew to a halt and Nina Vassilievna joined me in the body of the plane. "Are you sure Sherlock Holmes did not escape?" she asked.

I swallowed. "No," I said, shaking my head and finding that I was unable to speak further. Nina had half turned away, and held a handkerchief to her face. "We had better get out and report," she said gruffly.

I threw open the door in the fuselage and was confronted by an officer in the Royal Flying Corps pointing a pistol at me. Behind him, at the ready were some half-dozen soldiers, all with bayonets fixed. "Do you mind pointing those things in some other direction," I shouted, "We are English, you know."

Some little time later Nina Vassilievna and were sitting in the small hut used a combined living quarters and office by the airfield squadron commander. He introduced himself as Major James Lawson, and poured three large measures of brandy from a bottle he kept in a drawer. "I'm sorry your friend went down," he said. "I'd start a search, but if he went down on the other side there's not much hope. If he survived the crash they may have taken him prisoner, but I am afraid that that is unlikely."

I was mystified by this somewhat cryptic remark. "What on earth can you mean? Of course they will have taken him prisoner."

The Major poured himself another measure brandy and began rolling a cigarette. "Things are rather different here than anywhere else," he said in a dull monotone. "In the Flying Corps, I mean. For a start, the men on the ground are totally unable to distinguish between different types of aircraft. That means they shoot at anything that flies. When we cross the line we do it through a hail of small arms fire from the Germans and from our own chaps. You're just as likely to get a British bullet through your head as a German one.

"The next thing is that the soldiers hate aircraft. You can't blame them. They're stuck down there in the mud, penned in by barbed wire, with the enemy spraying them with machine-guns or pounding them with artillery, and then they have to contend with aircraft strafing the trenches or dropping bombs on them. It's bloody murder.

"When a plane comes down, if the pilot survives, he's likely to be shot out of hand, or worse still, bayoneted. A chap I was at school with, he was nineteen, two years younger than me, went down four days ago behind their lines. His propeller had been shot off, but he glided down to a perfect landing. I was flying with him and I followed him down to make sure he was all right. He got out of the plane and some Germans who had been excavating dug-outs nearby came running up. I saw him put his hands up, but it wasn't any use."

"What happened?" I demanded. "Did they shoot him?"

The young major sighed. "They killed him with a spade," he said, draining his glass.

The major made a telephone call to his headquarters and announced a few minutes later that a search was under way for Holmes and the prototype monoplane. In the meantime, Major Lawson detailed his mechanics to begin repairing the giant German plane so that it could be flown to London for examination by Mycroft Holmes's department.

Nina and I sat morosely in the squadron office next to the field telephone and waited for news of Sherlock Holmes. It was late in the afternoon when Major Lawson came into the office.

"I've just been over to Divisional Headquarters," he said. "They've called the search off. I'm afraid there is no sign of your friend. We must presume Mr. Holmes is dead."

Flight from the Front

Numbly I heard the major telling us he had made arrangements for our accommodation overnight. The giant German aircraft, he said, was ready to fly once more, and the smashed machine-gun had been replaced by one of British manufacture. We would be able to take it to London at dawn. I sat listening to the arrangements that he had made, but found myself unable to concentrate on any subject other than the death of Sherlock Holmes. At last I felt a comforting arm round my shoulders and, unresisting, allowed myself to be led away to my bed. It was only when I was between the blankets that I realised I had been brought there by Nina Vassilievna. She turned out the lamp before leaving me, but for hours, as it seemed, I could not sleep, for I was reliving the terrible events of the last twenty-four hours.

In the morning, however, I was awakened by an orderly with a mug of tea and an invitation to breakfast with the commanding officer. I accepted the tea, but turned down the invitation, for I felt no humour to meet other human beings.

A little later Nina knocked on my door. "We are able to take off for London now," she whispered softly. "Last night I sent a wireless message informing Mycroft Holmes of the danger at Heaven's Portal - that was of paramount urgency."

I gazed at her. "Is there no news ... ?"

Sadly she shook her head. "Nothing new. We must resign ourselves, Doctor. He is gone."

With a heavy tread I followed her to the field where our aircraft awaited us. As I did so, I remembered that same feeling of fearful depression some twenty-three years before when I found Sherlock Holmes's note above the Reichenbach Falls in Switzerland. Then he had written, "My career had ... reached its crisis, and ... no possible conclusion to it could be more congenial to me than this." Then he had referred to the defeat of the Napoleon of Crime, Professor Moriarty. But would this manner of death, that of an anonymous soldier in a foreign field, have been so satisfactory to him? I could not believe that it would.

Almost mechanical in my gait, I followed the footsteps of Nina Vassilievna and found myself sitting alongside her in the second pilot's seat of the giant plane. A member of the ground staff swung all four propellers and we were soon bouncing across the grass prior to becoming airborne. Of a sudden, I noticed Major Lawson running towards us waving his arms. Abruptly Nina shut down all four engines. It was only then that I could hear what the Major was shouting: "He's here. It's a miracle, but he's here."

My gaze followed his gesticulations, and there, beside the squadron office, standing next to a motor car which had obviously been his conveyance to the airfield, I saw a sight I had never dreamed I would see again. The tall figure of Sherlock Holmes waited there, his left arm shielding his eyes from the watery winter sun. He was alive!

I leaped down from the aeroplane and raced towards him, gripping him by the arm. "Holmes!" I cried, "Is it really you? Can it indeed be that you are alive? Is it possible you succeeded in escaping that awful aerial combat?"

"A moment, Watson," laughed Holmes. "It is certainly many years since you spoke thus to me. In '94, I think, when I returned after that affair of staging my own disappearance at Reichenbach."

"But how did you manage to escape?" I cried. "We gave you up for dead."

A quarter of an hour later, when Holmes had sent a further, more detailed report to Mycroft, he, Nina Vassilievna and I were on board the giant German plane flying towards England. With Nina at the controls, Holmes and I sat inside the fuselage. All three of us were wearing helmets connected by telephone and so were able to speak above the roar of the engines.

"I was almost over our lines when I saw you being beaten to earth by the attacks of von Richthofen and his cronies," said Sherlock Holmes. "So I turned back to give you what assistance I could. You had already accounted for one of your assailants by the time I arrived, and my appearance was enough of a surprise that I was able to despatch a second before they realised I was among them. After that, it was a little more difficult.

"I managed to dodge them for a while, and got in a few shots, but in the end their greater experience in their chosen craft began to tell. A shot from von Richthofen penetrated the engine of my plane, and I began to lose power and go down. In no time both of them were behind me, and bullets were tearing into the aircraft. All I could do was head towards a bank of cloud and attempt to evade them by hiding there. In part it was successful, except that I did not perceive that the cloud in which I was seeking cover was, in fact, ground mist. I found myself suddenly flying just above trenches, with little or no hope, due to the difficulties with the engine, of achieving a greater altitude. Finally I was forced to attempt to land. I was heading for the Allied lines at a height of something like fifty feet, and losing altitude fast. Suddenly, with some two or three miles to go, the engine cut out completely and I began gliding. Looking down I could see the German support trenches, and I realised I was going to land some quarter of a mile behind the German lines. However, it seemed that any likelihood of being recaptured was somewhat remote, since I considered that falling from that height and at that speed it was likely the crash would kill me.

"Fortunately it was not to be so. My machine ploughed into the sea of mud and shell-holes, there was a tearing, ripping crash and the aircraft seemed to close up around me. I was thrown forward and struck my head, and everything went black."

Sherlock Holmes smiled as he reached this dramatic point in his story, and paused before continuing. "I recovered a short while later to hear a broad Scottish voice offering me a drink of water. I opened my eyes and looked up at a somewhat anxious officer in the Royal Scots. At first he took me for a German, but I quickly convinced him I was as British as he."

"Yes, Holmes," I said, "But what was this officer doing behind German lines?"

"Obviously, Watson, we were not behind German lines. Although I had seen the German support trenches just before I landed, the Scots had made a sortie and taken the area minutes before I crashed. I concede it was somewhat fortuitous."

"Very fortuitous." Nina Vassilievna added her dry comment over the telephone link. "But what happened to the aircraft?"

"It was loaded on to a lorry and despatched to divisional Headquarters," replied Holmes, "there to await shipment to London."

The Albert Hall

Almost our first sight on landing at an airfield a little way to the south of London was the expansive smile on the face of Mycroft Holmes. As we climbed down from our aeroplane he advanced on us, arms spread wide. "Sherlock ... Dr. Watson ... what magnificent success! Asquith is delighted; His Majesty has been informed and is to invite you both to the Palace; the whole country, indeed, will soon be talking about your exploits. To have brought about the destruction of Von Bork, to have spirited our most fearless agent," this accompanied by a slight inclination from the waist to our companion, "away from the dangers of the German High Command, to have engineered the capture of more than twenty spies who had infiltrated this country, and not least, to have taken possession of two of Germany's most secret aircraft ... superb, Sherlock, absolutely superb!"

"Then Heaven's Portal has been cleared?" said my friend, waving aside the congratulations.

Mycroft nodded enthusiastically. "Indeed it has. Wiggins and his men were there at first light this morning ... but come, let us go to my car and I shall tell you the entire story as we travel to London." The four of us moved across the tarmac towards a large car parked on the periphery of the landing strip.

"By all accounts it was a completely successful operation, my dear Sherlock," continued Mycroft as we settled into our places and moved smoothly off northwards. "As I say, Inspector Wiggins and some hundred and fifty police officers converged on the village of Heaven's Portal just before dawn today; two observers from my own department accompanied the police, but it was thought more practical to have an operation of this sort dealt with by the civil authorities rather than the military. The private estate was effectively surrounded, and precisely at seven-fifteen Wiggins and forty officers, most of them armed for this special operation, forced entry into the main building at various points. Surprise, I understand, was absolute. Twenty-five Germans in all were arrested."

"One moment," said Holmes, interrupting his other. "Was there any attempt to resist made by the Germans?"

"That was rather a curious feature, Sherlock," replied Mycroft. "A few certainly tried to fight back, and some shots were fired, though nobody on either side was seriously injured. But most of the Germans seemed almost glad to see the arrival of our authorities."

Holmes mused for a moment. "Instructive," he murmured.

"But hardly surprising really, Sherlock. It was inconceivable that a mission on this scale could be expected to last more than a few months without detection. The various pieces of equipment captured together with the agents shows the range of activities they had been engaged in since they penetrated this island. Working constantly under so much pressure, trained as they were, I should not be altogether surprised to discover that a good many of them are fairly happy to end their war service. When we have obtained confessions from the ringleaders - to be frank, Sherlock, I am not looking forward to finding out what recent incidents can be attributed to their machinations - then they will be deposited in the Tower, there to await the outcome of the war. We cannot, of course, risk the consequences of execution: reprisals could be catastrophic. I am inclined to believe, my friends, that after a few questions, the details of the unfortunate explosion at a munitions factory in Manchester and the apparent chance wrecking of three naval launches in Hull harbour only a month ago, will come to light. We found quantities of explosives, rudimentary though effective timing devices, cameras, detailed maps, climbing equipment and a whole cache of clothing for disguises." I glanced at Holmes as his brother was listing this catalogue; he raised his eyebrows briefly, presumably at the scale at which the Germans had operated, but generally he did not appear unduly surprised. Nina, however, let our a low whistle of astonishment and commented briefly on the relative supply arrangements of German and British undercover agents. Mycroft Holmes acidly remarked that a submarine could not be sent to Berlin, then addressed some further remarks to his brother.

"Wiggins and his men also discovered some sizeable cages and stores of raw meat. That would tend to explain old Sloe's death, would it not?"

Holmes nodded. "That indeed corroborates my own thinking on the matter," was all he said.

"They were falcons," rejoined Mycroft. I expressed my mystification, but neither brother vouchsafed any explanation; indeed, the four of us remained entirely silent for the rest of our journey, each wrapped up in his or her own thoughts.

We reached Baker Street in mid-afternoon, to be greeted effusively by Mrs. Hudson, who acted as if she had not seen us for eleven months instead of eleven days. Mycroft left us, bidding us to meet him later that evening at the Albert Hall. "Full dress, remember, gentlemen," he said. "It's rather important affair, with almost the entire Cabinet putting in an appearance to show that we care about the plight of those refugees from Belgium."

Sherlock Holmes smote his brow. "Good Lord, Mycroft, in all this excitement, I had forgotten completely about the New Year's Eve concert! Yes, certainly, Watson, Nina and I shall be there: eight o'clock, is it not?"

Mycroft signified agreement and, bidding farewell to us all, returned to his car and was speedily driven off, doubtless back to his desk at the Diogenes to make final reports on the events in Essex that morning, and to press ahead with the questioning of the captured agents. As we made our way up the stairs towards our rooms, Mrs. Hudson laid a hand on Holmes's arm.

"There's Peter Wiggins upstairs, together with that young lady waiting to see you."

Holmes wheeled around in surprise. "Why, it must be Miss Dempster, the doctor's young friend! Well now, Watson, does that not bring an even happier ending to this case? Come, I have an apology to make to the young lady." He threw open the door to our sitting-room and we perceived Polly Dempster's grave young face as she sat waiting us beside a roaring fire; Wiggins sat slumped in a corner. They both rose as we entered. The girl spoke first.

"Dr. Watson, Mr. Holmes - how nice to see you both again. I hope you do not mind too much that I should be here to greet you. But ever since the day my uncle's body was found - it is already nearly two weeks ago - I have been looked after by a neighbour. Then a police officer, after he'd asked me some questions, thought that I would be safer if I left the village yesterday and I was taken up to London. I spent the night at Scotland Yard," she said proudly, brushing a wisp of brown hair from her eyes. "Then Mr. Wiggins here brought me to Baker Street; he has told me what happened in the village this morning."

Holmes crossed over to her and took her small hand in his.

"Now, you have been a brave and sensible girl through all this and I have just told my friend Dr. Watson that I must make a proper apology to you." Holmes settled down in his accustomed chair. Wiggins, who had still not spoken, idly moved a case from the wicker chair to permit him to sit down. The girl stood before Holmes, although not before glancing briefly in my direction, as if she did not know what my friend was going to say.

"When you came to see me," said Holmes, "I was rather rude and said some things which I now regret. It did not seem to me right that a young lady of your intelligence should insult me by trying to make me believe in old legends. But I now know that there were indeed some Hell Birds at Heaven's Portal, and they were altogether too tangible. Inspector Wiggins will have told you what happened in the village, that the private estate and manor house were taken over by some spies, men whom I and Dr. Watson have been chasing for the past two weeks. They were very clever men, Miss Dempster, and when they heard about the local story, they thought of a very clever idea and I am not at all surprised that you were deceived by it. So that the village people would not stray too close to the manor, they brought some specially trained falcons, which were set to fly around the perimeter of the estate and attack if anyone came close. That, I fear, is what your uncle did; and the birds had no hesitation, when they sensed that a stranger was near, in swooping down on him. Then, when his body was found with the claw marks in his skin - although I daresay a heart attack was the actual cause of death - people would say that the Hell Birds had carried out their deadly work and would be even more afraid to go outside in the night, and especially not close to the estate.

"When I saw the news of your uncle's death in the papers the day after you had come to see me, the doctor and I were already about to travel to Heaven's Portal when another, more immediately important matter had to be cleared up. It is likely that if I had come to the village on that Friday, I should have discovered the truth a little earlier than has actually been the case. But of course I could not possibly know that your uncle's disappearance and a cell of German agents could be connected." He ended his long talk and gazed into Miss Dempster's eyes.

She had remained silent throughout, hanging on my friend's every word. Then she spoke in a soft, low voice. "Thank you, Mr. Holmes, and you too, Dr. Watson: I don't know the lady here," indicating Nina Vassilievna. "It is still just a little difficult for me to talk about my uncle: I don't think we were very close, but we had looked after each other after the death of my parents. Inspector Wiggins told me that you have all helped to save the country and I am very proud to have known you and been even a tiny part of the adventure."

Holmes chuckled self-effacingly. "Perhaps saving the whole country is putting the matter on too high a plane, but we thank you, Miss Dempster. And it is now time not to pat ourselves upon the back, but to think of your future; we all have your interests very close to our hearts."

The girl seemed unsure of herself, after the pretty speech she had just made. "I don't know Mr. Holmes; perhaps I shall work ..."

"Come now!" interjected Holmes. "A young lady of your tender years shall not work if the doctor and I have anything to do with the matter. These are questions to be discussed tomorrow, however. For the present, Wiggins, I am sure you wish to tell me of the contents of this strange container you have brought?"

I looked across to the inspector. Wiggins cleared his throat. "It is nothing of any real importance, Mr. Holmes - merely something we found this morning that has no bearing on the case, but in which I thought you might be interested." He bent down and opened the clasp of the case he had moved from the wicker chair on our entrance. From inside he withdrew a violin and handed it to my friend.

"Indeed," said Holmes, turning the instrument over delicately. "As you say, rather a surprising object to have come upon in such a den. It is a fine piece of work - an Amati, no less, with a previous owner who, I perceive, was once a seafaring man. But the musical inclinations of a German spy need no longer concern us," he continued, returning it to Wiggins. "Rather, it is to our own musical pleasures tonight that we must look forward. Watson, I believe you have a request to make of Miss Dempster?" He looked across in humorous fashion.

"Me, Holmes? Why, I don't understand ..." I began to reply; but Holmes winked, and I understood his drift. "But of course ... er ... Miss Dempster!" I hesitated a moment. "Will you do me the great honour of permitting me to escort you to a concert at the Royal Albert Hall tonight? My friend Mr. Holmes already has a partner for the evening, I believe." Nina smiled in agreement. The Prime Minister will be there, together with many of the great men in the land; it is not, I think, an occasion to be missed and I would indeed be most honoured."

Her eyes glistened and her whole face seemed to light up. "Oh, the Albert Hall! And to go with you and Mr. Holmes! Oh yes, I should like that very much!" Thereupon, the remainder of the afternoon was spent in close consultation with Nina Vassilievna and Mrs. Hudson over what clothes the girl should wear for the occasion.

All disputes over costume had been happily resolved by the time we had to leave for the Albert Hall. Between them, the two ladies had managed garb Miss Dempster in a most attractive pastel affair that was well able to highlight her youthful looks. Nina Vassilievna too had miraculously found a fitting costume, and although it was she who held open the door of the official car that Mycroft had sent for us, it was clear that she could act as a true lady when it so suited her. Sherlock Holmes, in relaxed mood, expatiated during the drive upon the merits of Joseph Haydn as composer - I understood that there was to be one his symphonies played that night as the high spot of the concert. I had thought that Haydn, as a German, was not the most obvious of composers to have his works performed by a refugee orchestra, but I was quickly informed that I was mistaken.

"He was Austrian-born," explained Holmes, "and even spent several years in this country: he was granted a Doctorate of Music by my own University of Oxford." I was content with this surprising news.

The road skirting Hyde Park in front of the Hall was packed with broughams and chauffeured cars as we drew up, bearing witness to the class of audience attracted by the gala New Year's Eve festivities. Inside all was splendour. Superbly dressed ladies and their escorts promenaded in the corridors behind the auditorium; liveried servants moved smoothly among the throng of politicians and nobility, dispensing bottles of champagne, and the scene augured well for a most successful celebration. Nina Vassilievna took Holmes's arm, and Miss Dempster shyly took my own, as we were ushered by a most superior attendant down towards the first row of seats before the apron of the immense stage. It seemed to me that, despite the plethora of great names around us, attention was drawn to our small party by all who we passed. I heard on several occasions Holmes's and even my own name whispered in hushed tones, and I could not help but reflect with some pride that my accounts of our escapades had contributed in no little measure to the fame of my friend and the fact that he was so readily recognised. Holmes himself appeared unaware of the stir he was causing and talked quietly to his companion as we were shown to our seats. I was not sensible of the honour being done to us until I looked beyond Holmes and saw the Prime Minister, Mr. Asquith, deep in conversation with the Secretary for War, Lord Kitchener, and Mycroft Holmes, occasionally waving a hand through the air as he emphasised some point. When the Prime Minister saw Holmes, he advanced on him with an expression of delight and clasped him warmly.

"Mr. Holmes, I cannot commend you too highly for what you have done in spiriting this most brave young lady from the clutches of the Germans; your brother has already given me some indication of your adventures over the past few days, and I shall doubtless be receiving a full report from yourself in the near future. Tonight is not only New Year's Eve: we may reasonably regard it as an occasion for real celebration, both for the rescue of your charming companion and the total eclipse of the enemy spy ring in this country. This morning's operation at the village of Heaven's Portal was, I understand, a model of organisation and execution. I know some of my colleagues would wish to congratulate you also," he continued, steering a protesting Holmes toward a group of men I recognised as the most important members of Mr. Asquith's Cabinet. As Holmes was engulfed by them, the Prime Minister turned to me and spoke a few kind sentences, ending with words that it had so often been my lot to hear at the conclusion of a successful case. "Doubtless we shall be reading all the facts when you write the complete story for the *Strand*, doctor?" I made some non-committal reply, knowing full well that Sherlock Holmes would lay down an absolute prohibition on the publication of details of the business that had just ended. The young girl at my side was privileged to be presented to Mr. Asquith and he was able to find time to pass some words with her, adding immeasurably to what, I believe, had already become a great experience for her.

An usher passed a programme to me and I settled in my plush crimson velvet seat to peruse the details of our entertainment. The eighteen musicians and their conductor had managed to escape from Belgium only a few hours before the Germans invaded the country. In the succeeding months, after they arriving in England, they had spent their time in touring the country, performing in many towns, large and small, always to earn money that could be passed on to other victims of the atrocities in their small country. I pointed out to Holmes how they had traversed England to aid their gallant land: this night's concert was the culmination of a tour that had taken them, among other places, to Liverpool, Manchester, Leeds, Hull, Cambridge and Colchester.

"Certainly they are well travelled, Watson," was his reply as he studied the programme closely "Let us hope that their musical accomplishments are as fine as their appetite for our railways." At that moment, there was a buzz in the audience and a burst of applause greeted the appearance on stage of the refugee orchestra. The electric chandeliers that bedecked the hall dimmed slowly, and finally the players were engulfed in the only light that shone in the entire amphitheatre. I heard a soft sigh of happiness from Polly in the seat next to my own; then, with a histrionic flourish from the baton of the conductor, the celebratory concert was under way.

Each item was cheered to the echo as it ended and the capacity audience seemed in a mood to forgive every rudimentary error that the unsophisticated players made: they were, after all, a small orchestra from a country of no great musical tradition, and, while certainly talented, were undoubtedly unused to performing in such august surroundings. Nevertheless, they acquitted themselves with credit, and even Holmes, musical purist that he was, was moved to comment favourably in the interval. During that short period of relaxation yet more people insisted on introductions to Holmes and myself, and the ten minutes passed very quickly. Holmes, however, had now become uneasy at the degree of public recognition he was receiving, and I fancy he was glad when the lights went down for the second half of the performance. Haydn's Forty-Fifth Symphony was the only item to be played in this section, and I looked forward to an opportunity to retire considerably earlier than I had been used to of late.

Holmes leaned across to me. "I think you may be interested in this piece, Watson; I would draw your attention to the final movement." With that cryptic comment, he sat back and the music started. Soft and sweet it was: the Belgian orchestra had clearly rehearsed to perfection, since this was their *pièce de résistance,* and none of the mistakes made in the preceding rather more patriotic works was apparent. So smooth, indeed, was the performance, that I was amazed to see one or two of the members of the orchestra moving restlessly in their places as the last movement was in progress.

"What is happening, Holmes?" I murmured to my companion. "Why, two of the players are getting up and leaving!" Truly, it was quite extraordinary, but one of the oboists and a member of the horn section had risen from their seats and, laying down their instruments, passed down off the stage. I could see Holmes smile in the darkness.

"Hush, Watson," he whispered sibilantly. "That is what I meant when I told you that the final movement was interesting: Haydn wrote the piece in such a way that it is a tradition for members of the orchestra to file out as their parts end." As the movement progressed, so more players left, and I marvelled at the skill with which the composer had written the symphony so that there was no real musical loss despite the occasional disappearance of orchestra members. Within a very few minutes the stage was completely empty but for the conductor and two violinists. Then they too left the playing area and as the last strains of music lingered in the air, the conductor turned, bowed quickly and departed.

Next to me, I sensed Holmes stiffen in his seat and, throwing a quick glance in his direction, I saw his face contorted with perplexity. His left hand, that had rested hitherto on the arm of his seat, clenched tightly into a fist, and I was suddenly aware of immense suppressed excitement. Applause from the audience ascended in a crescendo and already calls were coming for the orchestra to return onto the stage to take another bow. Holmes's mouth dropped open and his eyes widened, as it seemed, in horror. Then, in an incredible instant, he was on his feet and bounding up on to the platform. I rose from my own seat, thinking that he had taken leave of his senses. He dashed to the centre of the stage and turned to face the thousands, some of whom were already faltering in their clapping and cheering. Polly Dempster, beside me, touched me lightly on the arm.

"What is Mr. Holmes doing?" I had not time to reply, for just then, Holmes's voice came stridently over the general hubbub.

"Clear the hall! All of you, to the back, quickly, for God's sake! Clear the front rows!" Mr. Asquith was on his feet, staring dully at my friend's frenzied form.

"What is this, Mr. Holmes?" he cried, and Mycroft attempted to clamber on to the stage to restrain his brother.

"Move! Now!" was Sherlock Holmes's only reply, shouted so

urgently and in so fearsome a tone of voice that people around us did indeed begin to stir in their seats. "Away, quickly! Your lives are at stake!", and then the rush started.

I stood aghast at the action, lunatic as it seemed, of my friend, but I had spent too many years with Sherlock Holmes not to know that his commands should be obeyed. I grasped Miss Dempster's hand in my own, and together we ran towards the rear of the auditorium. All around us there arose the most fearful din: ladies screamed, gentlemen swore as they dragged each other from their seats, attendants ran hither and thither, a uniformed policeman hurled himself against the storming tide of people running to the rear, trying to make his way down to the stage. Shouts, cries, screams echoed in the vast chamber; there was total pandemonium, and above it all, I heard Holmes call once more.

"Away, for your lives!" I turned for an instant and momentarily saw the lone figure of my friend hurling a violin case away from him and leaping from the stage to the deserted rows of seats before him. Then it seemed that a great noise filled the hall, the rending sound of a gigantic explosion; the passionate screams of all about me redoubled, a body fell on me and a wave of unconsciousness swept over me.

A Masterstroke

An age later I awoke, to find the anxious face of Polly Dempster looking down at me; and as I gradually regained awareness, I realised that I was back in Baker Street, stretched out on a couch in the familiar surroundings of our sitting room. "What ... what is this? What has happened?" I heard myself say.

In a moment, Sherlock Holmes was at my side, and, as he helped me to an upright position, I saw that there were others in the room - Nina Vassilievna sobbing in a corner, her dress ripped in several places, Mycroft Holmes seated by the fire, shaking his head, Inspector Wiggins from Scotland Yard pacing furiously around the room. "It's all right, my dear old friend," said Holmes in a soothing voice. "Everything is over and we have emerged unscathed."

"But what has happened, Holmes?" I said frantically. "It seems to me I recall a noise ... a furious sound that tore through my head. The concert..." Polly Dempster, on Holmes's instructions, administered a much-needed glass of brandy to me, and within a few minutes I was fully recovered.

Holmes took up a position before the fire, hands behind his back, pulling at the tails of his evening coat. "The catastrophe, I am glad to say, was not as appalling as it might have been. I can take little credit, other than that I saw what was happening and understood the situation a little sooner, perhaps, than my brother here." Mycroft Holmes shook his head in deprecatory bewilderment. Holmes continued: "When Mycroft reported the details of what had happened at Heaven's Portal this morning, I was left with a feeling of vague unease in my mind: I could not put my finger on exactly what it was that bothered me; there was perhaps one point above all that left me unsettled. Mycroft said that only a few of the German spies had tried to fight back when Wiggins and his men moved in. These were highly-trained agents of the Kaiser: there was much at stake if their cell was destroyed - individually, they might face death if they were captured and tried for spying. Why then was there only a token resistance? Perhaps there was an obvious explanation - Mycroft himself did indeed give a plausible reason - but I was not satisfied.

"We arrived back in Baker Street to discover Inspector Wiggins, accompanied, not only by Miss Dempster, but also by a rather fine and expensive violin. This, he told us, had been found during the raid on Heaven's Portal. I expressed some little surprise at the time; why, I asked myself, should dedicated German spies, on a secret mission in wartime England, liable to be in danger at any time, bring with them a violin, and no ordinary instrument at that? An Amati cannot fetch less than some hundreds of pounds. Indeed, why should they bring anything that was not entirely essential for their mission - they would, after all, have little time for amusement? A mouth-organ I could accept, but an Amati? I think not. Logically, therefore, the violin *was* essential for their purposes. This much I had deduced and yet, in the absence of any further indications,. I was left with a clue that had no tale to tell.

"When we arrived at the Albert Hall tonight, and I saw assembled the leading figures in our government, my thoughts returned to one of the sworn objectives of the German secret service - the assassination of the senior members of the Cabinet. One of the first things Nina told us was the Kaiser's decision to adopt such a policy of assassination. This New Year's Eve celebration would have been the ideal opportunity for such a horrifying blow to be struck; and yet I comforted myself with the thought that the would-be perpetrators of such an outrage had been languishing in the custody of our authorities since dawn this morning. Nevertheless, I could fit the Amati nowhere in the puzzle: it continued to disturb me - it troubled me for no apparent reason other than that it should not have been there.

"We came to the Albert Hall, then, under the impression that we would be witnessing a performance by a small group of brave men from Belgium, men who had left their own land at the last possible moment, and who were now spending their time in raising funds for brethren who had been less fortunate. What we saw instead was a group of nineteen enemy agents." I sat up in astonishment. "Yes, Watson, you may well look surprised," continued Holmes, "and believe me, the pieces did not come together until the maestro made his final bow and his exit from the stage.

"You, Watson, ever the conductor of light, gave me a further indication of the truth yourself, all unknowing. You read to me from the programme a list of towns that the orchestra had visited on their patriotic tour. Was it, then, coincidence, that among them were Manchester and Hull, towns that Mycroft had mentioned only a few hours earlier as having suffered unaccountable disasters, destructive to our war effort? What was it, Mycroft - an explosives factory in the one, the destruction of naval launches at the other? I believe those were the two incidents you recalled. In themselves hardly conclusive, but, taken with the other unanswered questions, instructive for all that.

"But their undoing came in their ignorance of musical tradition. Here we were meant to be at a performance given by one of the foremost small orchestras in pre-war Belgium, and yet they were apparently unaware how to play Haydn's Forty-Fifth Symphony. You may not know, Watson, that a tradition has grown up around that single piece of music; it has its own nickname, the 'Farewell Symphony.' Why 'Farewell'? Because the players, as their parts end, leave their places and move off the stage. Horn-players, then oboists and bassoonists make their exits: they are followed by the various strings players, until the conductor alone is left with the two principal violins. The piece comes to an end, they bow, and the other members of the orchestra return to the stage to take their bows also. But what was it that we saw tonight? The two violinists and the conductor left the stage, the latter after a perfunctory salute to the audience. A warning bell seemed to ring in my brain, and I fancy you, Watson, saw me moving uneasily in my seat. But a moment was needed for the facts to fall into place, all the disparate threads coming together in a blinding flash of understanding. The stage should not be left bare; why then had the violinists and conductor absented themselves? It was all wrong - it should not be thus. Why should they wish to leave the stage clear?

"Happily, I was able to furnish an answer to that question. In diabolical fashion, a plan had been laid, as Nina had discovered, to destroy Asquith and the Cabinet, all ranged in the first row at this patriotic occasion, in one cataclysmic moment. Every one of the instrument cases had been packed with a certain amount of explosives and held timing devices in them, so that after a measured time, they would detonate of themselves, devastating the front rows. It was a masterstroke to choose Haydn's symphony to cover the attempt: it was a perfect excuse for the perpetrators of the crime to leave the scene in complete order, and with no immediate suspicion falling on themselves. They knew to the second how long the symphony would last - they were thus able to set the timing devices to explode a matter of minutes after they had vacated the stage, yet while the audience was still on its feet.

"They did not, however, bargain for the true music-lover who knew, positively knew for a fact, that tradition demanded the last two violins remain on stage. I saw them move, I was unhappy, and I finally saw the truth. I was able, by my actions, to clear the front few rows of seats of the all-important targets for these desperate men, although I fear at least one usher at the Hall was severely injured by the impact of the blast. The escaping agents were all captured within minutes of the explosion. There was, of course, increased security at the Albert Hall because of the presence of the Cabinet, and I was able to alert the police quickly enough."

I was unable to contain myself any further. "Holmes," I expostulated, "you speak of agents; but what agents? Were there others aside from those arrested this morning? What has happened to the real Belgian refugee orchestra? Where are they?"

Holmes smiled. "Is it possible that you are still in the dark, my dear Watson? Can it really be that you still do not see the truth? We must put it down to the unaccustomed excitement of the past few days.

"A subtle and delicate operation was needed. This morning, Wiggins and his officers apprehended twenty-five men in Heaven's Portal. According to Nina's information, upon which we acted, the village housed a number of German agents; and Wiggins, quite reasonably, thought he had triumphed with these arrests. But I would commend a study of the languages of Belgium to you, inspector: these men whom you thought were Germans were in point of fact speaking Flemish, a language, I grant, superficially not unlike German - and those few who defended themselves were the guards left to look after them while their comrades travelled around the country, masquerading as the refugee orchestra. It was a *coup de maître,* clearly planned with infinite care and precision, to capture the entire genuine orchestra at the very outset of their tour, and continue in their guise throughout England. It was brilliant to make use of the legend of the Hell Birds of Heaven's Portal, and train falcons to attack any villager who strayed too close to where the real members of the orchestra were held prisoners. And always in their minds, the one ultimate aim: to destroy the Cabinet in one outstanding moment, a proof to other enemies of Germany that no one could stand up to their might and succeed. The gala concert set for New Year's Eve gave them their chance ... and who would suspect the orchestra?"

Holmes paused and leaned back against the mantel. The five of us were still, gazing at him in awed silence, although I fancy Mycroft had understood all the arguments his brother had made before he uttered them. "Is there any other point that eludes you?" said Holmes.

Polly Dempster stirred sleepily by my side. "They must have been very clever spies, all to be able to play as an orchestra?" Wiggins nodded in agreement.

"Perceptive, young lady, " rejoined Holmes. "And yet I am sure the inspector and my brother will find, when they come to interview these men, that just as they were not all in an equal class as agents, so they were not, every one of them, fine musicians. The orchestra was merely a vehicle, with real musicians whose talents tended toward the playing of an Amati, backed up by a smaller number of professional secret agents, who controlled the operation while taking on the guises of the tour organisers and officials: perhaps a few of them even took the minor orchestral rôles. Indeed, while the leading violinist exhibited tone and phrasing of the highest order, others in the stringed section showed a deplorable tendency to hash the tonic 7th in the third movement.

"Such a project, of course, would be difficult to mount: yet so important was the final objective to the Germans that little expense or effort would have been spared. I am sure that in Germany at this time, there was no shortage of patriotic musicians willing to lend their services to such an endeavour - doubtless, were it necessary, brother Mycroft would be able to engineer such an enterprise himself."

Holmes's brother considered the point, then nodded gravely. "It would not be impossible, Sherlock; it would not be impossible. And if we did mount an operation of a similar nature, it would have a rather more successful outcome, of course."

"How can you be so sure?" queried my friend.

Mycroft Holmes quivered with mirth. "Because there would be no Sherlock Holmes to thwart us!" he bellowed in explosive glee.

Holmes gave a cry of mock anguish as some drops of aged brandy spilled to the floor from Mycroft's shaking glass. "Brother, is this the steady hand that steers the ship of state?" Nina Vassilievna laughed merrily as Sherlock Holmes, glancing at the clock above the fire, crossed to the window and threw back the curtains. "Come here, all of you."

We clustered around this extraordinary man and, as he charged our glasses, the tolling of a thousand London churchbells signified the coming of the New Year. As one, we raised our glasses in a silent toast - a prayer for peace, an expression of hope.

Outside, the first snow of 1915 began to fall.